WALLY

WALLY

by
Judie Wolkoff

AN
APPLE
PAPERBACK

SCHOLASTIC INC.
New York Toronto London Auckland Sydney

*To Gene,
who's learned to live with
the animals I've brought home,
and Alexa and Justine,
who would welcome more.*

---

*With special thanks to Susan and Vern French of Small World's,
Inc., New York, whose expert advice in caring for real-life chuckwallas would never include a closet or a sun-lamp.—J.W.*

ISBN 0-590-40700-7

12 11 10 9 8 7 6 5 4   2 3 4 5/9

40

Contents

1
Getting Acquainted

Billy Wiggins said he had something important to show me, so I knew it was going to *be* important. He doesn't kid around. "Why don't we meet at my house after school on Wednesday?" he asked.

"Sure," I told him without getting an okay from Mom first. I had my reasons for not asking and they weren't because I knew she'd say, "Sure," or "Fine," or "Go ahead, Michael." She wouldn't. She's been suspicious of Billy since he gave me a horned toad last year. You'd have thought the world was coming to an end when she found it in her curler bag.

All I have to do is barely mention Billy's name and

1

she starts carrying on . . . like he's a gangster. And not your old, regular, everyday gangster, either. A big-time gangster: El Numero Uno on the F.B.I.'s Ten-Most-Wanted list.

To avoid a scene, I ended up telling her to expect me home a little late from school on Wednesday. "An hour or so," I said. "I'll be working on a science project."

You might call that information a little misleading, but you can't call it a fib. Reptiles are definitely a part of science and Billy definitely has reptiles . . . Not only do his parents *let* him raise them . . . they *help* him raise them. They even bring them to him from wonderful places like swamps and deserts. Even jungles.

As far as I know, Mr. Wiggins has never made a trip anywhere without bringing back something scaly for Billy, which is one of the reasons why the two of them finally had to build a big greenhouse behind their garage. It never was meant for flowers, but it still took almost a whole summer to fit the sheets of glass together and put in a heating system — and was it ever worth it! Reptiles love the place. What's more, I can't think of a kid around who wouldn't give his eyeteeth for a chance to go in there. Except for maybe Marvin Oates. I always figured that drip would faint if he saw a worm.

"My backyard at 3:15 sharp," Billy said when I met him during recess on Wednesday. We synchronized our watches, checked them and double-checked them, then we wound them up twenty times.

2

With that kind of organization and planning ahead, something was bound to go wrong. Naturally. My class got out ten minutes late, so I ended up running like crazy all the way to Billy's house.

"Not bad," he said when I came barreling around the corner of his garage. "It's only 3:16." He was holding a chocolate-covered donut and he handed it to me. "Here's yours . . . I ate mine already."

I took a couple of big bites, thanked him, then neither of us wasted any time before going inside the greenhouse. As usual, the place was jammed with all of his pets. "Hey, you've got a whole new batch of chameleons," I called to Billy as he headed toward the rear.

"You can look at them later," he called back. "Come on down to this end."

I edged my way in between all of the cages of geckos, salamanders, and snakes to get over the big cage where he was standing. Then he moved to the side so I could get a good look.

I have to admit that I was counting on something pretty spectacular, but I sure wasn't ready for a big, black thing with rust-colored blotches and a long, thick tail that hung over the side of its rock. It just sat there very quietly ignoring us, so I crouched down beside the cage to get a better view.

If it was a lizard — and I wasn't sure that it was — then I'd never seen one like it before. Ever. Still, I had this strange feeling that I knew it from somewhere.

That head. That small, funny-shaped head. It seemed so familiar. So did the long neck and the short forelegs and the big hind legs.

"How'd you two like to get better acquainted while I go get his lunch?" Billy asked.

I didn't answer. I was too busy studying this what-ever-it-was I was supposed to get acquainted with. More than anything else, those big hind legs were getting to me. They *really* reminded me of something I was sure I'd seen before.

Only where? I wondered. Was it in a movie? On TV? Could it have been a picture? In a book maybe? Then it hit me. I had seen a picture of it . . . in my dinosaur book. *I was staring at a trachodon!* No doubt about it. I've read that book so many times I can tell you *exactly* how trachodons looked, how many teeth they had, how big they got, and what they ate.

What d'ya know, I thought, Billy's got himself a trachodon . . . an extinct pet. I looked this one right in the eye. Even though it hadn't moved a muscle, I knew it was as much alive as I was. Which shows how much you can trust paleontologists who write things about trachodons dying out millions of years ago.

"He's a vegetarian, isn't he?" I called to Billy.

"Yeah . . . how'd you guess that?" he asked when he came back with a brown paper bag.

"I didn't have to guess," I said. "I know he's a vegetarian, because I know what he is."

"You do? *Wow* . . . that's incredible." Billy shook his head. "You have no idea how unusual you are, Michael. There couldn't be another kid in ten million who'd know."

"You really think so?" I asked.

"I really do," he answered. "One kid in ten million."

I looked back at the trachodon. "What does he have . . . about two thousand teeth?"

"Nope . . . no teeth. Just little crunchers."

Crunchers? Of course. How silly of me, I thought. This trachodon was only a baby, probably just hatched. He'd get his teeth when he was grown. Adult trachodons have two thousand teeth.

I looked up at the greenhouse ceiling. It was high, but not high enough for a pet that was going to get two stories tall. "What are you going to do with him when he grows up?" I asked.

"He is grown up. Two feet's about as big as a chuckwalla ever gets."

I felt my face drop. "A chuckwalla?"

Billy's face dropped too. "Yeah . . . I thought you knew."

"Knew?" I said. "Of course I knew. I just thought you'd have some kind of *unusual* name for him, that's all. It sort of took me by surprise hearing you call him 'a chuckwalla' . . . like he was plain. Ordinary."

"I call him 'Wally.' I figured it was either that or 'Chuck.' "

"Wally, huh?" I said, looking back in the cage. "Where'd you get him?"

"Arizona. Dad had a job taking pictures in the desert down there, and he found him. Isn't he the most terrific lizard you ever saw?"

I nodded, even though I didn't think he was nearly as terrific as a dinosaur. Still, I was dying to get him to walk over to me, but he just sat quiet as ever, guarding his rock.

"Do you like him?" Billy asked.

At that, Wally who hadn't even noticed me before, perked up his head and started staring right through me with those beady little eyes of his.

"Yeah, I do," I answered. "I think I could love him."

Billy reached inside the paper bag he was holding and pulled out a handful of grapes. Carefully he pinched off the stems, then began tossing them, one at a time, into the cage.

"How'd you like to take care of him for three or four weeks?"

I stopped crouching. "Did you say three or four weeks?"

"Yeah," Billy said, "about that long."

"About that long, huh?"

Billy nodded.

I usually don't stand around sounding like somebody's echo, but what else was I going to do? Forget that I lived with my mother, Catherine the Reptile-

6

Hater? Forget the rotten way Catherine the Reptile-Hater had threatened to skin me alive if I ever brought anything home from Billy's house again?

Billy was waiting for an answer.

"Well," I stalled. "Starting when?"

"Next week. Dad has to go back to Arizona . . . to take pictures of Navajo and Hopi ceremonies this time, and he wants all of us to go with him."

"What about school?"

"What about it?" he said with a big smile. "My teacher thinks it's a great idea. She says I can show the class all my slides when I get back."

Wally lumbered over to the grapes, then munched one while he listened to us talking. It was for darn sure he wasn't some cute, cuddly little thing that Mom wouldn't mind having around. On the other hand, I'm not the kind of person who's going to let something starve just because it isn't some cute, cuddly little thing. Wally slurped down another grape and when he looked at me again, it was in such a way that I just knew he was counting on me to say yes.

"Why not?" I said.

Billy gave me a pat on the arm, then looked in the cage. "Did you hear that, Wally? You're going home with Michael. And Michael's going to get a book with a picture of you in it."

"What book is that?" I asked.

"This one right here," he said, reaching into a box of

books near Wally's cage and handing me the one on top. "Dad's latest. Take a gander at page forty-one."

I glanced quickly at the iguana on the cover and read: *How to Live with a Lizard* by W. I. Wiggins. Then I opened it to page forty-one. "Hey, you weren't kidding," I said, looking at the picture, then Wally, then back at the picture again. "It's really him."

"Yeah . . . terrific picture, huh?"

Before I had a chance to come up with another "terrific," Billy was looking over my shoulder. "You can skip that part about where to get a chuckwalla. Read the other stuff." He ran his finger down the page. "Right here . . . where it says, 'If you bring a chuckwalla home, you must remember that it is a desert animal and needs heat. Lots of heat.' " Billy stopped reading. "You don't have to worry about that. We'll give you a heating fixture when your mom and dad drive you over to pick up the cage."

"Mom and Dad?" I almost choked on the words. "They won't have to come . . . I already have a cage."

"Left over from the horned toad?"

I hate lying to a friend, so I didn't say anything. I just nodded.

"Heating system too?"

I nodded.

"*Super!* Then you're all set to go. Why don't we read the section on food?"

I looked at my watch. "It's pretty late, Billy. Would

you mind if I read about it at home?"

"Okay . . . go ahead. If you have any questions, just give me a call. Anyway, I'll see you at school. Want to meet at recess tomorrow?"

"Fine," I said, closing the book. "Recess . . . tomorrow." I glanced at the iguana on the cover again. "He looks interesting."

Billy smiled. "If you have a minute, I'll show him to you."

I turned to follow him and somehow my belt buckle got caught around a wire on Wally's cage. When I pulled back to loosen it, I practically knocked the cage over, sending Wally flying down to one of the bottom corners.

Billy helped me get free and once we straightened the cage upright again, Wally scooted behind his rock and began puffing himself up like a balloon. "Hey," I yelled. "What's he doing?"

"Don't worry," Billy told me. "He's just protecting himself . . . that's all. Chuckwallas always do that when they're upset or they think they're trapped."

"Blow themselves up?"

"Yeah. If they're wedged in between something, they can't be pulled out."

I slid my belt around so the buckle was back in the front and looked at Wally. "Well, I sure hope he's his old normal self before I come to pick him up."

"He will be," Billy said, tugging at my elbow. "Let's

go see the iguana while he cools off."

After Wally, the iguana was a disappointment. So were the chameleons, the geckos, and everything else in the greenhouse. Except the tarantulas.

"Wow, are they hairy," I said to Billy.

"And fun," he told me. "That's why I have them even though they're not reptiles."

"Who's taking care of them?" I asked.

"I don't know yet. Everything's boarded out but the two of them and a snake. You know anybody who might be interested?"

"What about Marvin Oates?" I asked.

I meant Marvin as a joke, but Billy didn't laugh. "Not a bad idea," he said, rubbing his forehead and looking very thoughtful. "Not bad at all. If Marvin had something better to do with his time than practice penmanship. . . . "

"And spelling," I added.

"Yeah, that too . . . Who knows . . . he might just turn into a halfway decent person." Billy started laughing. "I almost forgot to tell you something," he said.

"About Marvin?" I asked, thinking he'd finally caught on to my joke.

"No, about Skeeter. He's taking care of the chameleons for me, and when he came over to see them yesterday, I showed him Wally and. . . . "

We were at the greenhouse door.

"Yeah," I said, slipping the book under my shirt so

10

Mom wouldn't spot it. "Go on."

"... Skeeter thought Wally was a trachodon! Can you believe that? *A baby trachodon!*"

I looked back at Wally who was still puffed up in the corner of his cage. "No kidding," I said.

2
The Snoop

Halfway through dinner that night, Mom asked me how my science project was coming along. "Oh, all right," I said, hoping there wouldn't be any more questions. No such luck. My nosy brother Roger wanted to know what my project was. "Just something in the dinosaur line," I told him while I studied a forkful of green beans I had absolutely no interest in eating.

Dad cut into his pork chop and looked up. "Well, Catherine, at least we know that's something that won't be coming home for live study." Then he turned to me. "Right, Michael?"

"Mmmm," I mumbled as I shoveled the beans in my mouth and tried chewing. "Right."

Across the table Mom eyed me coolly. "He wouldn't

dare bring anything home . . . not after the episode with that horrible horned toad." Her face softened a bit and she gave me a little smile. "That's why you chose something extinct, isn't it, dear?"

"Uh-hmmm."

It's amazing how long you can work on a mouthful of beans if you really have to. I'd probably still be sitting in that chair if it hadn't been for one of my Sister Snaggletooth's famous belches.

The minute our dinner conversation shifted from my science project to her manners, I quickly excused myself to go upstairs and do my homework.

When I got to my room, I sat on my bed and started thinking about how I was going to keep Wally around for three or four weeks . . . sight unseen.

Not having a cage meant finding a hiding place that was not only big enough for him to move around in, but warm enough too. Hot, in fact.

Oh, I know I'd told Billy I was all set up, and he thought I still had a cage from the horned toad. But the truth is, that toad wasn't around long enough to get a cage. He'd never really had a home except for Mom's curler bag and my bed.

"You busy?" Rog called while he knocked on my door.

"Yeah," I answered, then wondered why I'd even bothered. He seems to forget we're not sharing one big room anyone. We've had separate rooms since Dad put up a partition a few months ago. We even have our own private doors going out to the hall, and mine has a KEEP OUT sign on it. But Rog always ignores it.

As soon as I saw the knob turn, I dashed to my desk and pretended I was doing my homework. "Let's see," I said, scribbling on a piece of paper, "59 goes into 3,643 . . . uh . . . "

"Sixty times," he answered for me. "Just round out the 59 to 60. I thought you learned that last year."

"I did," I said, "but this has decimals in it. Anyway, can't you read signs?"

"What signs?"

"Oh, never mind. What d'you want?"

"I need to borrow your globe."

"It's on one of my bookshelves," I told him without getting up. "Look for yourself, I'm busy. Let's see . . . 59 goes into 3,643 . . . *point* 398. . . . "

I should have known that he wouldn't just find the globe and leave me in peace. "Hey, Michael," he chirped, "you planning on getting another horned toad?"

I dropped my pencil and spun around in my swivel chair just in time to catch Mr. Snoop looking through the book Billy'd given me. "Put it back," I said.

Roger has a habit of ignoring me. *"Wow!* Did you ever see anything like this before," he said, squinting at one of the photographs. "It looks just like a dinosaur."

14

I jumped up and grabbed the book. "Scram," I said and handed him the globe.

Instead of leaving, he just stood there looking at me. "Betcha I know what your science project is all about," he said as a rotten, know-it-all grin spread across his face.

One thing about my brother Roger is . . . *if* you let him in on a secret, he'd probably go through a torture chamber and not let it out. Another thing about my brother Roger is . . . *if* you *don't* let him in on a secret and he finds out about it, he's got one of the biggest mouths in town.

"Rog," I whispered, trying to sound friendly, "can you keep a secret?"

"Cross my heart, Michael. Is Billy giving you a toad or a chameleon?"

"Neither. A chuckwalla."

"A chuckwhat?"

"A chuckwalla. The same one you were just looking at in the book."

"The very same one?"

"The very same one. That's his picture. His name's Wally."

Roger started jumping up and down clapping his hands. "Why didn't you tell me before? This is terrific. Sensational . . . and Mom's just going to kill you."

"Mom's not going to find out," I said, "Because I'm going to find a place to hide him in for a few weeks."

"For a few weeks? Aww, that's all? I thought Billy was *giving* him to you."

"Nope. I'm just taking care of Wally while Billy's on vacation."

"Vacation? It's not even summer yet."

"You don't have to rub it in," I said. "Just help me think of a good hiding place . . . that's warm."

"What about our bathroom . . . it's warm in there. We could keep him in the tub."

"What about Snaggletooth?" I asked. "She happens to use our warm bathroom."

"Right," he said. "What about . . . hmmm . . . "

There was another knock on my door. "I'm doing my homework," I called, but Snaggletooth doesn't read signs either.

"You're wanted on the phone, dummy," she said when she walked in.

"Me?" Roger asked.

"No, the other dummy. Michael."

"Keep thinking about how we can round off 59, if you know what I mean," I said to Roger. "I'll be back in a minute."

"Right," he said, winking at me.

"What's *he* winking about?" Snag asked.

"Nothing," I answered, following her out the door. "He's got something in his eye. Who's on the phone?"

"Billy Wiggins. And I already told Mom."

I picked up the hall phone since I thought Mom was downstairs. "Hi, Bill. What's new?"

"All kinds of things," he answered, just as Mom conveniently loitered by with a pile of laundry.

"Like what?" I asked, watching her stop a few feet away.

"Well, for one thing, Michael, I won't be able to meet you tomorrow at recess . . . I'll be home packing."

"A week early?"

"Not anymore . . . the trip's been moved up to Friday. Dad wants to be in Arizona in time for a Hopi ceremony, this weekend."

"This weekend, huh?"

"Right. Think you could pick Wally up a few days early?"

I craned my neck to see how Mom was doing with the towels she was unloading one at a time into the linen closet. "Could you be a little more specific?" I asked.

"Sure. How about either tomorrow or Friday?"

"The 'or' sounds better," I said.

"The *or?* You mean Friday?"

"Uh-uh."

"Fine with me, if you can get over here right after school . . . say by 3:15? We have a five o'clock flight."

"Righto," I said, looking over at Mom who was now stacking a bunch of washcloths.

"Got any questions about the chapter on chuckwallas?"

"Uh-uh. I finished my . . . uh . . . homework be-

17

fore you called. No problem at all with it."

"Terrific," Billy said. "So I'll see you Friday at 3:15. Oh, one last thing . . . Marvin's taking the tarantulas and the snake."

I mumbled something like "how nice," and when I got off the phone I went whistling down the hall past Mom.

"Well, I rounded out 59," Roger told me when I reached my room.

"Whew . . . it'd better be a good one," I said, shutting the door and leaning against it. "Things are getting tight. Billy was on the phone just now, and he's not leaving next week. He's leaving this Friday! *The day after tomorrow!*"

"So soon? Yow! We'd better hurry and get the washing-machine ready then."

"The washing-machine," I yelled. *"That's* what you spent all this time figuring out?"

"Yeah, don't you think it'll work?"

I flopped on my bed and closed my eyes. "How did I ever get myself into this?"

"Okay," Roger said. "If you don't like the washing-machine idea, how about a closet?"

"Which one?" I asked. "We have them all over the place . . . the kitchen, the halls, the bedrooms. There must be *at least* eight."

We narrowed our choice down to two: mine or his.

"Mine's bigger," he said.

"But it's not in *my* room."

"Mine's still bigger."

"But it's *still* not in my room."

"Oh, all right . . . go ahead and have it your way. Keep him in your closet."

"Thanks," I said.

"You're welcome," he answered in a big huff. "And what are you going to do? . . . Just leave him on the floor in there?"

"Nope. We need a box. Have you got one?"

"I might," he answered.

"Look, Roger, do you or don't you?"

"Well, I said I might. What about my train box?"

"Perfect. Why don't you go get it?"

"It has my train in it."

"Empty it," I said.

"And what do I do with the cars and the tracks and the control switches and the houses and the cross guards and . . ."

"*Stop!* We'll just have to find a place to put *them* in."

"Want to start now?" he asked.

"No, we'd better wait till the coast is clear. Get ready for bed and when everybody's sleeping I'll tap three times on the partition. That means empty your train box. When you're finished, *you* tap three times back and I'll come help you put everything away."

"Three taps. Gotcha."

3
Setting Up

I don't know whether I took my bath and got ready for bed too fast, or whether everybody else was just too slow. One by one, I heard Snag, and Rog, then Mom go to bed, but it seemed like I waited forever before the third stair from the top creaked. It always creaks if you step right in the center of it, and Dad always steps right in the center of it. Especially when he comes upstairs at night.

I listened to him walking down the hall turning out the lights, then I heard a door close. Good, I thought, he's finally going to bed. I propped up my pillow, and while I was lying there waiting for his snoring to start, I looked over at the partition and wondered what Roger was doing on the other side. He's the type who can manage to make noise just taking his pants off, so I usually know what he's doing even if I can't see him. But he wasn't making any noise, and I was afraid he'd be zonked out before we had a chance to set anything up.

Fifteen minutes went by, and I got out of bed and tiptoed down the hall. The snoring was loud and steady . . . so I quickly tiptoed back to my room. When I got there I heard Roger rattling around. "Hey," I whispered through the partition, "what're you doing? You were supposed to wait till I tapped."

"Then tap," he whispered back. "Dad's snoring . . . I can hear him."

I tapped three times and Rog started rattling around again. In a few minutes he tapped to me. "Just stay there," he whispered. "The tracks are already in my shoe bag and everything else is under my bed. I'll come to you."

When he brought the box in, I was clearing things out of my closet to make a big space for it on the floor. "Push it in here," I said. "I'll try and slide it behind my clothes rod."

"Okay, but none of your pants and shirts are long enough to hide it."

"I know that, so get busy and find something to cover the side that's showing."

"How's this?" he asked, handing me my dart board.

I propped the dart board along the side of the box. "Perfect . . . except for this corner. See what else you can find."

There wasn't anything else bigger than a roller skate, so I hung up my robe and Rog helped me drape it over the end of the box.

"If you ask me, it looks suspicious," he said when we were finished.

"Are you kidding? Mom would need X-ray vision to see your box."

"That's not what I meant," he said. "It's your robe. She's going to think something's awfully funny when she sees it hanging up."

"Don't worry. I've done it before. Twice, in fact."

"Okay," he said with a shrug. "If you say so. Now what?"

"The sun-lamp," I said.

"What sun-lamp?"

I reached under my bed. "This one. Wally needs heat, so we've got to hook it up."

"When did you bring *that* in?"

"After my bath. And *nobody* saw me. So don't ask."

The two of us got on our knees and groped around in the closet trying to find a place where we could hang the lamp so it could shine in the box without burning up my clothes.

"What about halfway up this wall back here?" Rog asked.

"Still too close. It'd get my baseball uniform."

Roger sighed. "Are you *sure* Wally needs heat?"

"Positive," I answered. "He's a desert animal."

It took a while, but we finally came up with a perfect spot for the lamp on a side wall in my closet. The worst part was screwing the hook in, because it needed a couple of smacks with a hammer to get it started and I had to time them *exactly* with Roger's coughs.

When the hook was screwed in and I was just about finished hanging up the lamp, Rog thumped me on the shoulder. "Hey, Michael, where are you going to plug it in?"

I sat back and looked around the baseboard of the closet. "How could anybody be so *stupid*?" I groaned.

"You're not so stupid," Rog said. "Anyone could've made that mistake."

"I wasn't talking about me, dodo. I was talking about the architect who planned this house. There's not one socket in here."

"Aww, heck," Rog said, throwing his hands in the air. "Why don't we forget about the sun-lamp? Somebody might want to use it . . . then what'll we do?"

"Nobody's touched it since Dad cooked himself. Remember?"

"Well, we still can't plug it in."

"We can if we get an extension cord."

I crept quietly down the stairs and got the one that was in the den. When I brought it back upstairs, we plugged the sun-lamp into the cord and strung it around the floor of my closet. Then we made sure it was flattened under my rug and stretched it across the room.

"Darn," I said, after I'd pulled it as far as it would go. "It just misses the socket . . . by two feet."

"Maybe there's a closer socket," Rog said.

"There isn't. I've already checked. This is the closest."

"Maybe we have another extension cord."

"You can forget that too," I said. "This is the only one in the house and what's more, I give up. I *quit*. Wally won't have heat."

I thought Roger would be thrilled, but he wasn't even paying attention to me. "I've got it," he said, jumping up and down, "I've got it. A brilliant solution."

"Pipe down," I whispered, "or you're going to wake everybody up."

"You wait . . . this idea is *brilliant*."

"Where are you going?" I asked.

"Downstairs. I'll be back in a jiffy."

"All right," I sighed. "Just don't step in the middle of the third stair."

He did. I half expected Snaggletooth to come charging out of her room to tell Dad there were robbers in the house, but somehow she slept through the creak. *And* the next one, when Roger came back upstairs.

"You're not going to believe how brilliant this is," he said, puffing into my room.

I know from past experience that Roger's ideas are rarely brilliant, and when I looked at the carton of Christmas tree decorations he was carrying, I knew this wasn't going to be one of those rare moments.

"Just you wait," he told me as I sat down on my bed and watched him unload. Within seconds he was surrounded by tinsel, stars, homemade styrofoam snowballs with toothpicks sticking out of them, and a sickening-looking string of popcorn that somebody had forgotten to throw out.

"Look, Rog," I said, trying to be very patient, "if you think you can fool Wally into thinking it's winter with all that stuff, you're wrong."

Without listening to me, he kept digging into the carton. "Wouldn't you just know these would be packed way down at the bottom?" he said, pulling out a string of lights and dragging them into the closet.

I didn't even bother following him in there to see what he was up to. I knew it was hopeless, so I just settled back on my pillow to read a comic book.

A couple of minutes later he jerked the comic book out of my hands. "Want to come see?"

When I got up and walked over to the closet it was almost blinding. Blinking off and on all around the rim of the floor were a couple of dozen colored Christmas tree lights, and above them, glaring straight into the train box, was the sun-lamp.

"Nothing to it," he said. "I just plugged the lamp into the colored light extension . . . then plugged that into the extension cord." He pointed over to the socket where the cord was plugged in. "We had enough left over to make it to the next socket."

He was looking so pleased with himself that I almost hated spoiling things. "Just one question," I said. "How are we going to keep Wally a secret when his hiding place is lit up like a carnival?"

"Well, if you really want to know, I thought about that too. We'll just turn on his heat at night when everybody's sleeping. Maybe we could call it . . ." Rog stopped talking and his face turned white. "Oh-oh, somebody's coming!"

"Quick! Get into the closet and stay there," I said, as we heard a sharp rap on my door.

"What's going on in there, Michael?" Dad called.

I quickly shoved all the Christmas decorations inside the closet with Roger and closed the door behind him just as Dad opened mine.

"Why, hi, Dad," I said. "Can't you sleep?"

"Never mind me. Why aren't *you* sleeping?"

"Ooh," I answered with a funny little squeak, "I'm doing some homework."

Dad looked at the comic book on my bed. "Some homework. And what's all the racket I keep hearing? Running up and down the stairs and . . ."

"I was hungry," I said.

"Two times?"

"Yeah, I guess so."

He looked down at the floor. *"What's that?"*

Out of the corner of my eye I could see the lights blinking on and off through the crack at the bottom of the closet door. "What's what?" I asked in my new squeaky voice.

"This," he said, stooping down, then coming back up with a handful of loose popcorn.

"Popcorn," I said.

Dad shook his head. "It's a miracle you don't get deathly sick from some of the junk you eat." He looked back in his hand. "Good Lord, Michael . . . this stuff is *vile!"*

"It really didn't taste too bad."

He threw the popcorn into my wastepaper basket. "No wonder you were coughing so much."

"That's why I had to go downstairs a second time. I needed some water."

"Hmmm. And what was all the pounding about?"

"What pounding?"

"The pounding on the wall."

"Oh, that. Well, you see, there was this, um, bug, and it was . . . um . . . crawling up the wall and . . . I smashed it."

"Once should have done it."

"It was a big bug . . . huge." I climbed to the top

end of my bed and leaned over my headboard. "It fell down there. Want me to find it? I'll show it to you."

"No, Michael. I'm not in the mood to look at a smashed bug. I just want you to get to sleep."

"Sure," I said, climbing under my covers. "I was just about ready to do that."

"*Now.*"

"Okay, Dad. Good night."

He stopped by my door to turn out the light. "It beats me how Roger could sleep through all this."

"Oh, you don't have to check on him, Dad. Really you don't. Listen . . . see? No noise. You'd know for sure if he was up."

Dad smiled. "Well, maybe that partition is more soundproof than the two of you let on."

After he left, I waited until he had enough time to get back to bed, then I tiptoed over to the closet.

"You can come out now," I whispered.

"I'll tell you one thing," Rog said, opening the closet door and wiping the sweat off his face. "I'm sure glad I'm not a desert animal."

"You could've pulled the plug out of the sun-lamp, you know."

"That occurred to me," he said, fanning himself with my comic book. "But I decided it was a lot better to melt than make a noise."

"Yeah," I sighed, "I guess you were right. Just make sure you don't so much as breathe when you go back to your room. Okay?"

"I won't," he said, "but I still have to tell you what we can call our bedtime heating system."

"What?" I asked.

"S.L.S.T."

"What's that?"

"Sun-Lamp-Saving-Time."

4
The Night Before

*T*here was a lot to be done when Rog and I got home from school the next day. Wally was coming in twenty-four hours, so not only did we have to finish setting things up, we also had to know what to do with him, and how to sneak him into the house.

"C'mon, we're gonna go dig a hole," I told Rog as I carried our croquet set out to the backyard.

Rog tagged behind me, yammering all the way about the time we were wasting and how a hole was never going to help us with anything. "If you ask me, this is ridiculous," he said when I stopped to pound a mallet handle halfway into the ground.

I wiggled the mallet around, making the hole bigger, then I pulled it out. "I'm not asking you," I said, packing a mound of dirt on one side of the hole." Then I sat back. "There . . . that ought to look like a burrow."

"A *burrow?*"

"That's what I said. It belongs to the mole you're gonna see tomorrow afternoon."

"Since *when* have we had moles?"

"Who cares as long as you can convince Mom and Snag you've seen one?"

Rog brightened up. "Ahh, now I get it . . . a *pretend* mole. And you want me to have them out here looking for it when you bring Wally home, right?"

"Right."

"Y'know, that's not bad, Michael. Not bad at all. What time do you want them out of the house?"

I thought for a minute. "Let's see . . . Billy asked me to be at the greenhouse by 3:15. It'll probably take me ten or fifteen minutes to talk to him and pick up Wally, then another ten minutes to walk home. Hmmm . . . you'd better tell them at 3:35."

"Three-thirty-five," repeated Rog.

"On the dot. The last thing I need is Mom greeting me at the door."

"Settled," Rog said. "Now . . . what else do we have to do?"

"Get a couple of rocks for the train box."

The rocks weren't hard to find since we have tons of them all over the hill at the back of our yard in Mom's rock garden. Rog and I picked out two of the biggest ones we could carry, and he was first to bring his inside. But not without crabbing about how heavy it was and how it was going to give him a hernia. At least no one saw him going to my room.

I wasn't so lucky.

"Hey, what're you doing with a big rock?" Snaggle-tooth asked when I passed her coming down the stairs as I was on my way up.

"I need it for a paperweight."

"Ha. You can't fool me. You're going to put it in your rock collection . . . that's what you're going to do."

. . . I looked down at her from the landing. "Now *how* did you ever guess that?"

"Because the only rocks you *ever* put in it are ugly ones, and *that's* ugly."

I didn't say a word. I just went to my room, slammed the door behind me, and took the rock to my closet. Roger was busy lining the train box with newspapers and when he seemed satisfied that he had enough, we put the rocks on top. "Those ought to make Wally feel right at home," I said.

"Yeah," Rog agreed. "Why don't we turn on the lights so we can see what it looks like."

I was disappointed. It still looked like two big rocks sitting on some newspapers inside a train box in the back of a closet that was all strung up with Christmas tree lights and a sun-lamp. "It'll have to do," I told Roger and pulled out the plug.

"*Wait*," he said. "I know what would help. A desert diorama. A *nighttime* desert diorama . . . all blue and purple with a few coyotes off in the distance. I'll start working on it right now."

I looked at my watch. "Too late. It's almost time for dinner."

"Then I'll do it after dinner."

"You can't. We've got to run through the chapter on chuckwallas again."

"Fine with me," he said. "I'll just sketch it out during math tomorrow."

All through dinner I kept waiting for Big Mouth to tell everybody about the ugly, gray rock I was adding to my collection.

"How big is it, Michael?" Mom asked, when she finally did.

"Huge," Snag butted in.

Without going into detail, I asked Mom if I could have a few words with her in private when we were finished eating. Then as soon as we were alone, I told her the rock wasn't really going in my collection. It was going behind my door . . . to barricade it. "I have to use something," I said, "Snaggletooth is . . ."

"Please don't call her that, Michael."

"Whoops . . . it sort of slips out every now and then."

"Not every now and then. You say it all the time. Now what were you telling me about your door?"

"That I have to barricade it if I want to get any homework done."

"I see. Because Susan's always bothering you?"

I nodded. "Yeah, and tonight's homework is really important. Not for me. For Roger. He needs a lot of help."

"Oh, what with?"

"Long division with decimals in it."

Mom put the last dish in the dishwasher and looked up. "And you're going to show him how to do it. How sweet of you, dear." She kissed the top of my head and told me to run along. "Don't bother with the rock," she called after me. "Susan won't come near your room. You have my word."

Roger was sitting on my bed thumbing through the pictures in *How to Live with a Lizard*. "Was Mom onto anything?"

"Uh-uh," I said, sitting down next to him. "She thinks we're doing homework."

"Well, in a way we are," he said, flipping through the pages until he came to the chapter on chuckwallas. Then he flattened the book across his knees so we could both see it and turned to the section on food.

I just skimmed over the things that were recommended, but Rog stopped to think about everything on the list like he was studying some sort of menu. "It's hard to believe," he said when he was finished, "but tomorrow night at this time we'll actually be feeding Wally." He looked at me, knitting his eyebrows. "What do you think we ought to give him for his first dinner . . . cactus flowers?"

"Uh-uh. Mom's cactus only has thorns."

"Oh." He looked back at the list. "How about some fruit?"

"Yeah . . . fruit's good for him, and I know he loves grapes."

Rog smiled and cupped his hands under his chin. "How does he take them . . . one at a time?"

I nodded, then turned to the next page. "Here's something we don't have to worry about. Exercise."

"Heck no," said Rog. "He'll get plenty of it just running around your room." He looked down at the paragraph on companionship. "No problem with that, either. That's us. Anything else?"

"This," I said, reading the next heading, HOW TO CLEAN THE CAGE. "It's the only part we haven't gone through."

"Why don't we just skip it? He's using a box."

"But it still has to be cleaned . . . and somebody's got to do it."

Rog read the first few sentences. "Y'know," he said, "it might not be such a bad idea if we included Snaggletooth."

"Forget it."

"But we could let her change . . . "

"I said forget it."

"All right. That about takes care of everything, doesn't it?"

I closed the book and Rog just sat there looking like he was off in another world. Finally he said, "Wally must be so cute when he sneezes salt out of his nose.

Have you ever seen him do it?"

"Uh-uh."

"Maybe he'll do it tomorrow." He put his head on my pillow and closed his eyes. "Would you mind telling me about him just one more time?"

"Well," I began, "he's about two feet long. And he's black with sort of rust-colored blotches on his back . . . and he doesn't drink water, and he doesn't sweat . . . "

"Keep going."

"And he has tiny little claws, a mouthful of crunchers, and he looks an awful lot like a baby trachodon. Oh, I almost forgot . . . he stores fat in his tail. Even from lettuce."

"Tell the part about how he looks up at you."

"Well, he's got these beady little eyes, and sometimes he half-shuts them with his eyelids. And when he looks up at you . . . "

"Yeah, that's the part . . . "

". . . he tilts his head to the side and blinks."

Rog sighed. "He sounds so wonderful." For a while he lay there with a dreamy look on his face, humming to himself. Then he opened the book to Wally's picture. "I just can't believe it," he said over and over. "I'm finally gonna meet him in person."

5
"3:35 on the Nose"

"Well, Michael Norman Price," I said to myself after breakfast Friday morning. "There's no turning back now. It's full speed ahead."

The box was all set up for Wally. The hole in the backyard actually looked like a burrow. And as far as I could tell, there wasn't a thing we'd overlooked. I'd even planned Wally's first meal: a banana, since we didn't have grapes, and it was already sitting on my windowsill getting ripe.

The only thing missing was Wally. Or at least that's the only thing I thought was missing till Rog, Snag, and I were racing out of the house to make the school bus.

"Michael," Rog said as he looked down at my lunchbox, "are you really going to bring him home in *that?*"

I didn't say a word. I just stepped off the curb to see how far away the bus was, then I tore back to the house. "See if you can get the driver to wait," I called to Roger. "The bus is about two blocks away."

"I'll try," he answered. "Better just grab a pillow-case."

The last thing I needed was Mom giving me the third degree about why I was going off to school with a pillowcase, so I ducked inside the garage to hunt for a gunnysack.

Our garage has so much junk in it that it's hard enough trying to find the car, let alone a gunnysack. But I knew we had to have some, somewhere. Every time it freezes, Mom has enough to wrap one around every plant in our yard.

I searched everywhere. Under tools. Behind bicycles. In back of tires, hoses, a couple of boards . . . even a big bag of charcoal. By the time I finally came across a whole pile of sacks in the wheelbarrow, I could see the bus from the garage window. It was just pulling up at the corner, so I grabbed the top sack, and ran.

"What's that stuffed in your jacket?" Snag asked as I clambered onto the bus behind her and Rog.

"A sweater."

Rog stopped on the top step and looked down at me. "A *sweater,*" he yelled. "How do you expect to bring . . . "

"Just keep moving," I said.

"Bring *what?*" asked Snag.

"A sweater."

"I *know* that. What're you bringing *in* the sweater?"

I hurried down the aisle with Roger and we took the first vacant seats we could find to get away from her.

"Can't you answer a simple question?" she asked as she squeezed in between two friends in the row ahead of us.

"Okay," I said. "Books."

"Books?"

"Right. Books."

Snag looked at me for a minute. "Y'know Michael," she said before she finally turned around in her seat, "you're even dumber than Roger."

"I hope you at least brought a pullover and not a cardigan," Rog whispered.

"I didn't bring a sweater, I just told *her* that."

"Oh, good. Then you did get a pillowcase."

"No, something better." I unzipped my jacket and pulled out a corner of the gunnysack. "This."

Roger frowned. "But isn't that going to be awfully scratchy?"

"Oh, don't worry," I said. "I'll make it. I've got a shirt on underneath it, so it's not really touching my skin."

"You? Who's worried about *you?"* he asked, just as somebody way in the back started yelling.

"Hey, Price . . . I hear you got the dinosaur."

Rog and Snag turned around to see who it was, but I didn't need to. I'd know Skeeter's voice anywhere.

"Hey, Price," Skeeter yelled again.

I slid further down my seat.

"Price . . . do you hear me?"

I closed my eyes.

"Hey . . . Roger-Dodger, poke your brother."

"He's sleeping," yelled Roger.

"NO HE'S NOT," Snag yelled. "I'LL GET HIM FOR YOU." She leaned over the back of her seat and lifted up one of my eyelids. "Michael," she said, peering straight into my eyeball, "Skeeter Magraw is in the back and he thinks you're getting a dinosaur."

I turned around and tried smiling at Skeeter while I waved to him. Then I cupped my hand over my ear. *"Can't hear you, Magraw. . . . Meet me at lunch."*

He gave me the A-Okay sign, and I slid back down in my seat and waited for the longest bus ride in history to be over.

When it was, I waited for the longest morning in history to be over so I could meet Skeeter at lunchtime.

But I didn't. Not with Snaggletooth bumping into me every ten seconds.

"Hi, Michael," she said when we saw each other for the umpteenth time in the playground.

"You again?"

"Yeah . . . have you seen Skeeter? I'll help you find him."

" I'll find him by myself, so quit following me."

"I'm not following you. I just wanted to ask you a question."

"What?" I asked as I cut through the middle of a basketball game.

"What did Skeeter mean about the dinosaur?"

"He was talking about my science project, and I said, '*Quit following me.*'"

Snag dodged a ball. "I'm not following you. I just wanted to know why he said you were *getting* a dinosaur?"

"Look," I said, wheeling around, "he didn't say *getting*, he said *got*. I *got* a dinosaur as a project. It was given to me . . . assigned to me. That's what he meant by *got*."

"Oh, shoot . . . is that all?"

"That's all."

After that, she didn't follow me around anymore. But then she couldn't. The bell started ringing and we both had to line up with our classes.

As mine was going upstairs, I saw the one person I'd really wanted to see, but hadn't, since we'd gotten off the bus together. Roger.

"Make sure you tell Mom I'm staying late to work on my science project," I whispered as I passed by him. "And be out at the burrow by 3:35."

"Three-thirty-five on the nose," he said, as his class made a sharp right turn to go down the hall to his room.

When I got to mine, I had the whole afternoon to sit

at my desk and panic. Would Roger be smart enough to remember everything? The most I could do was hope the answer would be yes . . .

That, and shift a dirty, scratchy gunnysack around under my hot, sweaty jacket while I waited for the last bell.

As soon as I heard it, I dashed off to Billy's house as fast as my legs would carry me. It was only 3:12 when I got to his driveway, so I slowed down enough to catch my breath, then walked around the front of his garage. Skeeter was coming around from the back.

"Hey, Magraw," I yelled. "I looked all over for you at lunchtime. Where were you?"

He was shuffling along, carefully balancing a small wire cage, and before he could answer my first question, I had another one for him. "How'd you make it over here so fast, anyway?"

He looked up with a grin. "Would you believe my teacher thinks I'm seeing the dentist?"

"She let you out early?"

"Yep. That's why I wanted to talk to you. I thought you could try the same thing and we could come over here together."

"Darn," I said, "I wish I'd known." Then I bent over to peek in his cage. "So you got the chameleons, huh?"

"Yeah, if I was taking home what you're taking home, my mother would kill me." He blew a long strand of hair out of his eyes. "You wouldn't believe what I had to go through just to get these. I even promised to practice my violin."

"Not every day, I hope."

"Yeah, every day. But don't worry . . . I'll still have time to play ball tomorrow. Want to meet in the park?"

"Fine," I said. "The usual time?"

"The usual time."

I looked at my watch. "Well, I'd better go now."

"Okay," he called after me. "But tell me something . . . how'd you know Wally wasn't a dinosaur?"

"His color," I called back. "Dinosaurs were army green."

"Good thinking, Price."

Billy was standing in front of the greenhouse holding Wally. "Hi," he said when he saw me. "We thought we'd wait for you out here. . . . See?" he said to Wally. "What'd I tell you? Right on time."

"Can I hold him?" I asked.

Billy nodded. "Let's go inside first. If he gets loose out here, it might be hard to catch him."

I followed him into the greenhouse and when he closed the door, I held out my arms. "I've never held a chuckwalla before. Is this how you do it?"

"Hmmm, maybe you'd better get down on the floor, Michael. I'll put him next to you and we'll see what happens."

I laid down on my stomach and he set Wally beside me. "Hello Wally," I said. "Remember me?" Wally

43

stared at me for the longest time.

"It's me . . . Michael," I said, giving him a hint, but he just sat there like he was glued to the floor. "Nothing's happening," I said to Billy.

"It will. It just takes time, that's all. In a couple of weeks you'll be like old buddies."

"Well, Old Buddy," I said getting up, "are you ready to come home with me?" I unzippered my jacket and pulled out the gunnysack. "I brought this for you."

"He's not going to like it much," Billy told me when I held the sack open.

I watched him carefully lower Wally to the bottom. "Why? Do you think it's too scratchy?"

"No . . . his skin's tough. He won't mind that. He's just going to be mad because he can't see anything. Besides there's nothing solid to walk on."

Wally started bouncing around and I had to gather the sack into a big clump at the top and hang onto it with both hands. "Is he mad now?"

"Probably, but he'll get over it as soon as he's in a nice warm cage."

"That's good to know," I said, looking all around the greenhouse so I'd keep my mind off the train box. Then suddenly I realized that something was very different. The greenhouse was bare. Empty. The cages were gone except for Wally's and two little ones. "When did everybody else get here?" I asked Billy.

"Oh, most of the kids came by yesterday. Marvin's

the only one left and he should be by here any second to pick up the tarantulas and snake."

I looked at my watch. Three-twenty-nine. "Well," I said, "I'd shake hands with you, but I can't, so have a swell trip."

"Thanks," Billy said, walking me outside. "I'll send you a card. . . ." Then he stopped. "Hey, I almost forgot . . . his vitamins." He slipped a small box into my jacket pocket. "It's a powder, so just sprinkle some on his food when you think of it."

"Okay. I won't forget."

"I know you won't. You two are going to have a terrific time together."

He waved good-bye as I crossed his backyard with Wally swinging at my side. "Feed him some flower petals," he called after us. "That is, if your mom won't mind giving up a rose or two."

"Righto," I called back, "as soon as they start blooming."

About halfway down the first block I saw Marvin. Usually I just turn around and go the other way when I see him. But this time, unfortunately, I had no choice. It was either pass right by him, or never get home.

"Did you get something from William?" he asked when he saw the gunnysack.

"You mean Billy?"

"No, I mean William. I hate nicknames. They're for the hoi polloi."

Marvin always tries to trap me with one of the fancy words he's picked up, and I knew this hoy-poy-whatever was one of them, so I ignored it. "I've got a chuckwalla."

"Oh, really," he said rolling his r and l's. "Well, I'm getting two tarantulas and a snake."

I had a sneaky suspicion that the reason he let the word *chuckwalla* go by with "oh, really" was because he didn't know what one was. "Marvin," I asked, "do you know what a chuckwalla is?"

"Of course I do," he snapped.

"What?"

"I don't have time to discuss it right now. I'm supposed to meet William." He started walking away then he looked back at me. "I got one hundred percent in spelling today. What did you get?"

"A hundred."

"No you didn't," he said with that snooty voice of his. "You missed four. I saw your paper."

It was 3:39 when I got to our front door because that stupid Marvin had loused up my schedule by two minutes. I tucked Wally, sack and all, under my arm, turned the knob, and went inside . . . praying that no one was going to be there.

Everything was quiet. A good sign. Even if Roger hadn't been smart enough to remember everything, he'd still come through for me. I took the stairs two at a time and when I was almost to the top I felt my right elbow slowly rising to the ceiling. "Okay, you can knock off your balloon tricks," I whispered to the blimp wedged under my arm. "You'll be out of there in less than sixty seconds."

Wally was still puffed up when I put him inside his box, so I took the banana off my windowsill and gave him a little piece that I sprinkled with vitamins. "Pretend it grew in the desert," I said. Then I left him alone to test out his rocks and calm down a bit, while I went out to join in the mole hunt.

6
"Widdle Pweshus"

"*I* don't think you ever saw one," I heard Snag whine as I crossed the backyard.

"Isn't *that* proof?" Rog yelled. "If a mole didn't make it, just tell me who . . . I mean what . . . did. Go ahead, tell me!"

The two of them were sprawled out on the grass peering into the hole and Mom was standing behind them bending over it. "Hi, Michael," she called when she looked up and saw me coming, "just getting home from school?"

"A couple of minutes ago," I answered. "I just dropped my books off upstairs. What's happening?"

"Oh, Roger!" Snag said with disgust. "He's been seeing things again."

"I have not," he shouted, "and how many times do I have to keep telling you that?"

"Ssshhh," Mom said. "You don't have to shout."

"Then why doesn't anybody ever believe me?"

Mom sighed. "I do believe you, dear," she told him as she wandered off to see how her rosebuds were doing. "It's just that we've been waiting almost fifteen minutes for this mole to come out . . . and I don't think it's going to while we're all here."

"Or *ever*," Snag added.

Roger looked up at me and grinned. "Think Mom's right?" he asked. "Maybe we ought to go in now . . . we could do something like clean your room or hang up your clothes."

"Not me," said Snag, "I'm not moving till I see how deep this is."

She started to stick her hand in the hole and I jerked it away. "You should *never* do that," I yelled. "You might get bitten."

"Ha. By what?"

"By something with rabies!"

She sat back on her heels and shrieked. "Is that true, Mom?"

"Don't drag me into this," Mom called from over by the fence, "and don't expect me to stay out here all afternoon listening to the three of you fighting, either. I'm going shopping and if any of you want new sneakers you'll leave with me now."

"I'm coming," Snag said, jumping up. "And this time I want the ones with stars and numbers on them."

"Then go wait in the car while I run inside and get my pocketbook." Mom headed for the kitchen door and when she got there she turned, looking back at Rog and me. "Well . . . are the two of you coming or not?"

"Gosh, Mom," I said, "I'd really love to come, but I've got an awful lot of homework."

"Yeah, Mom," Rog chimed after me, "I'd better stay and do mine too."

"Okay, it's up to you."

As soon as the door thumped behind her Rog got up and ran for the house. *"Wait,"* I called.

"Why?" he asked, reeling around. "Did something happen?" He stared at me with his mouth wide open till I caught up with him, then he put his fingers in his ears. "No . . . don't tell me . . . I don't wanna hear it. You either lost him or he got out of the sack or he isn't upstairs or Billy gave him . . ."

"Oh, stop it," I said. "He's up there."

"He is? Well, what're we waiting for?"

"For Mom to leave. And don't look too anxious . . . nobody runs to do homework."

Just then Mom walked out the door with her pocketbook. "Well, did you change your minds?"

"No," I said, dragging my feet, "we're just going upstairs to get started now."

"I think that's wonderful. You boys are really buckling down to your studies these days." She waved to us from the driveway. "Bye now . . . Susan and I should be home in an hour or so."

I waved back to her and when I turned around, Roger was gone. He'd left the kitchen door open and as soon as I stepped inside, I could hear him charging up the stairs yelling, "I'm on my way, Wally. I'm on my way."

I took off after him and by the time I got to my closet he was kneeling over the box so far he was practically falling into it. "Now I des wanna get an iddy-biddy peek at dis pweshus boy in here. Yes I do . . . Ohh ho, yes I do. You des so pweshus. Yes you are . . . ohh ho, yes you are. You des da mose pweshus sing Unka Rogie ever saw. Yes you are, ohh ho, yes you are."

I almost threw up. "Aww, knock off the baby talk, Rog. He's a full-grown chuckwalla, and it's not going to work."

"You wanna bet? Just take a look at him."

"I can't. You're in the way."

He shifted one-trillionth of an inch to the side of the box. "See what I mean. Is that the biggest smile you ever saw?"

"Oh, for Pete's sake," I yelled. "You're still in my way, but I can tell you right now . . . without even looking . . . that's *not* a smile. It's the way his mouth is shaped."

"It's a smile if I ever saw one."

"Yekk. Make a fool of yourself. Go ahead, but if you keep on insulting him like that he's *never* going to let you touch him."

Roger pulled his head out of the box. "What d'ya mean, he's never going to let me touch him? I've been holding him since I got up here . . . see," he said, carefully lifting his arm. "He's sitting in my hand."

I could have keeled over. Old Wally, who'd never done anything more than blink for me, was plopped in the palm of Roger's hand with his legs and tail hanging over the sides like he'd never been so comfortable in his life.

"He's so friendly," Rog said. "And I just can't get over the way his belly feels . . . almost like a pancake, it's so flat and round on the bottom. Weren't you surprised when you felt how *hot* it was, Michael?"

"Oh, I don't know," I said, hating the two of them, "were you?"

"Yeah, I sure was. I was surprised about his skin too. I never thought it'd be so soft . . . kind of silky." He held Wally up to his face until they were so close they were practically rubbing noses. "You des pweshus. Yes you are." Then he giggled. "You des twyin' to lick Unka Rogie's face now, aren't you?"

"He's *not* licking," I said. "He's smelling you. Can't you ever remember anything? The book says they *smell* with their tongues!"

Roger looked at me. "What're you so mad about? Be-

cause you think I'm holding him too long? Well, *here*
. . . if you're going to be so rotten about it . . . you
take him."

He held Wally out to me and the minute I picked
him up he did a flying leap into the air, landed on my
shirt, skidded all the way to my pants, ran down my
leg, and then scooted across the room to hide under my
bed.

"You know what I think," Rog said, going after him.
"I think he doesn't like your attitude."

I didn't say a word. I was in a state of shock. And I
mean *real* shock. It was like I'd seen a rock or a statue
suddenly come to life and start running around and doing all sorts of acrobatics. Oh, I know Wally had moved
his jaw a bit when I saw him eating grapes, and he'd
puffed himself up a couple of times. As far as that goes,
he'd even bounced around in the sack when I brought
him home. But move like that? Actually *leap* in the air
and then go hightailing it under my bed, when I was
beginning to wonder if his legs ever worked or not.

"Dere, dere Pweshus," Rog gushed, as he crawled
out from under my bed clutching Wally like he was
protecting him from some horrible ogre. "Michael says
he shorry, and Unka Rogie's not donna let him scare
hims Wally *enny*more."

He stroked the loose folds of black skin around
Wally's neck a few times, then he stood up, letting
Wally cling to the front of his shirt. "I think he's still a

little bit sore at you, Michael, for bringing him home in that gunnysack. Mind if I take him into my room and show him around? Maybe he'll forget about it?"

"Fine," I said, "but would you quit telling him I'm sorry? I'm not. I didn't do anything."

Rog shook his head. "You'll never change, will you? You *always* think you're right."

I watched them leave and in a couple of minutes the grand tour started going on next door. "And here's Unka Rogie's bed, and here's Unka Rogie's desk, and here's Unka Rogie's closet . . . and here's Unka Rogie's shoebag with all the choo-choo train tracks in it, and here's Unka Rogie's rocket that he made all by himself. Aww, you like it? You wanna go in it? Des lemme put da widdle pweshus in dere, den."

It got very quiet and I pressed my ear against the partition to find out what was going on. All I heard was Roger laughing like he was really enjoying himself. "Dere now," he said finally, "wasn't dat funsy-wunsy, Pweshus?"

The "pweshus" stuff was getting to me. I fiddled around my room doing a few things by myself, like clipping my nails, so I wouldn't have to listen to it. Then I looked in the box to see if Wally had eaten any of the banana I'd left for him. Of course, he hadn't. There wasn't a speck missing and it was in exactly the same place where I'd left it.

"Boy did he ever like my room," Rog said when the two of them came back. "We had so much fun."

He stretched himself out on my bed and let Wally sit on his chest so they could look at each other. "He's really beautiful, Michael . . . especially his head."

"Well," I said, "it's different."

"I *happen* to think it's beautiful."

Instead of arguing, I got the rest of the banana off the windowsill. "Here," I said, handing it to him. "You're gonna flip when you seen how beautiful he looks when he's chewing."

Roger unpeeled the banana in a hurry and I gave him the vitamins to sprinkle on it. "Does he like bananas?"

"Loves them," I said. "He gobbled a chunk right out of my hand before."

Rog broke off a little piece. "Come on, Pweshus, mash it up for Unka Rogie."

Wally sat blinking and I couldn't wait till he did another flying leap and scooted away. Instead, he perked up his head and waddled right over to Roger. "Hey, you're right," Rog hollered, "he is crazy about them. Look at the way those little crunchers are going to town. Isn't that cute?

"Oh, yeah. Adorable."

When Wally'd demolished the rest of the banana, he started wandering around my bed and I lifted up a corner of the bedspread, so he could go underneath. Naturally Rog thought it was the funniest thing he ever saw. "Can you believe that, Michael?" he asked when Wally lumbered right across the bed and came up over on his side. "He knew exactly where I was."

"Amazing," I said, watching him laugh his head off.

Then suddenly he stopped laughing and looked at me. "I *hope* you're not going to try sleeping with *him*."

"Of course not," I snapped.

"Well, maybe *you've* forgotten what you did when you rolled over on that poor horned toad . . . but *I* haven't."

I hoped this last comment would be the end of a subject I don't particularly enjoy talking about, but Roger has a one-track mind. "Bet ya never told Billy the truth about that, did you?"

I started to walk away but, he circled around in front of me. "Ewww . . . ickk," he said, scrunching up his face. "Do you still wear those same pajamas?"

7
Trying Out Sun-Lamp-Saving-Time

Roger and I tried being our old regular selves during dinner Friday night. Maybe he was a little more cheerful than he should've been, and maybe I was a little too grumpy, and I shouldn't have told Snag to shut up and go jump in the lake the tenth time she showed me her ugly new sneakers with the stars and numbers on them . . . but other than that, we acted pretty much the way we always do.

Except for one thing. I did watch Roger a lot. I couldn't help it. I was dying to find out what Wally saw in him.

What in the world was it, I wondered. What could he possibly have that I didn't have? Was it the way he smelled? Did he have some awful odor that lizards liked? Maybe he needed a bath? I tried smelling his arm when he reached across my plate, and I was sure the bath was the answer, but I kept my thoughts to myself, and nobody suspected, even for a minute, that something funny was going on.

Well, almost nobody. Snag did think it was strange that both of us wanted pears for dessert.

"Pears?" she asked. "You want *pears?*"

"Yeah," I said. "Pears."

"But they're fruit. And you *hate* fruit. You always say it isn't fair when we have it. *Always.* I've heard you."

"I changed my mind. I like pears."

"Me too," said Roger. "We think they'll taste great while we're doing our homework."

I think Mom was so thrilled at the prospect of having us eat something halfway decent for a change that she didn't seem to care what the reason was. She didn't even seem to care that we were taking food upstairs, which is only one step below reptiles on her list of pet peeves. "Just take napkins with you," she told us without going into her favorite speech about how a fleet of ants was going to invade our house. "And when you're finished, bring the cores down here and put them in the garbage."

"We promise," I said, grabbing a couple of paper napkins.

Roger had been in such a rush to make another big hit with Wally, that he'd raced upstairs ahead of me. When I got to the closet Wally was already sitting on his shoulder, like he couldn't get close enough to that old razzle-dazzle Roger smell.

Finally the two of them noticed me. Or at least one of them did. "Hi, Michael," Rog said. "I've told him about the pears."

"So?"

"So, now I don't know what to do."

"So give him a pear . . . you told him you had it."

"Whole?" he asked. "He's not a person, you know. How's he supposed to pick it up?"

Neither one of us had brought anything to slice the pears with, and since Unka Rogie couldn't bear the thought of disturbing his little "pweshus" while he went searching, I had to do it.

"Don't you have anything better?" he asked when I handed him my scissors.

"What d'ya think I keep in my desk . . . swords and bayonets? Look, you have two choices, Rog: you can either use those or smash it into chunks on one of the rocks."

Roger tried the rock, and when he had pear splattered all over the newspapers and dripping down the sides of the box, he gave me back my scissors. "Here. Maybe you'd better try cutting yours, Michael."

I'd barely had time to slice one dinky piece before the rest of the household decided to move upstairs, and Snag started pounding on my door. "Hey Rog, you in there with Michael? Cuz if you are, there's something you ought to know."

"Tell her I'm not here," he whispered.

"No," I said, dragging him out of the closet. "It isn't safe. She'll be in here anyway. See . . . what'd I tell you. There she is."

The door creaked open and Snag poked her head in. "I knew you weren't doing any old homework . . . and hey, what's *he* doing in your closet?"

Rog kicked the closet door shut with his heel. "I wasn't in there. I was just closing it for Michael."

"Ha," she said, walking around my bed to get a closer look at him. "And what's *that*? It's all over you."

Rog looked down at his shirt and arms, then started wiping them off with his napkin. "It's his pear," I told her. "It rolled on the floor and he fell on it."

"Fell on it? In your *closet*?" She turned from me back to Roger. "Boy are you a weirdo . . . *nobody* falls on a pear. Especially on his *head*. See that? You've even got it in your hair."

"So what," I said. "He hasn't had a bath for a long time and he needs one anyway." I nudged Roger. "You're gonna go in the bathroom and take one, right now, aren't you?"

"Oh, no, he's not," she said, racing to get out of my door. "He took his first last night . . . and the night before that! It's *my* turn, which is the reason why I came in here to begin with . . . so I could tell him."

She slammed the door, then opened it again. "What's more, you've been using *my* bubblebath . . . haven't you?"

"I have not," he yelled. "I don't even know where it is."

"Did you?" I asked as soon as Snag went out again.

"Did I what?"

"Did you use her bubblebath?"

"A little . . . so what's wrong with that?"

"Nothing. I just wanted to know what kind it was."

"I don't know. Just plain old bubblebath. She hides it in the cabinet under the sink."

"What does it smell like?"

"I think it was apples . . . no, peaches. Yeah, that's what it was. Peaches."

"Well, Rog," I said, patting him on the back. "Maybe you'd better not use it anymore. Somebody might make fun of you if you go around smelling like peaches."

"I'm more worried about the pear," he said, picking a piece off his eyebrow.

After he left, I waited for both of them to finish with their baths, then I went in. And sure enough, right in the back of the cabinet, hidden behind the bars of soap and all the ammonia and junk, was a bottle of Peach Delight Bubblebath.

The instructions said to pour in one capful, but I poured in three, and when the bubbles were up to the top of the tub, I climbed in. "So *this* is the answer," I thought while I practically drowned in the stuff. "Old Wally likes the smell of peaches."

I'd hardly dried myself and gotten into my pajamas when Mom started making her bedtime rounds to say good night and make sure the napkins and cores were down in the garbage.

The minute she left, Dad came in. "Isn't your homework finished yet?" he asked.

"Nope," I said, since I hadn't even started on it.

"Well, I'm going to bed now, and I don't want you up too late. You've got the whole weekend to do your homework. No bug smashing either . . . okay?"

After he left and I was sure the goodnight rounds were over, I hurried into the closet so Wally could get a few whiffs of my Peach Delight and start falling in love with me for a change. "How does this grab ya?" I asked, fanning my hand over his box.

There was absolutely no movement behind the two rocks, so I squeezed in closer and wiggled my fingers in the space right over Wally's head. "I said, 'how does this grab ya?' " Still no movement.

I must have sat there ten minutes waiting for him to come crawling out like I was the King of Peaches. He didn't though, and I finally decided to start him on S.L.S.T. and try again later.

Then I got into bed and watched the colored lights blinking off and on around my closet. I'd left the door wide open so I could see them, and I liked the way they looked . . . all nice and twinkly, like it was Christmas instead of the beginning of May.

But I didn't have a chance to enjoy myself for long: maybe thirty seconds or so, before Rog sneaked into my room to spoil it all. *"Psssssst,* Michael?" he whispered, "can I sleep in here with you?"

"No, and I told you before I wasn't going to sleep with Wally, so stop spying."

"I'm not spying, I just want to be closer to him, that's all."

"You can get closer to him tomorrow . . . in fact, you can spend the whole weekend in the closet if you want, so get back to your own room."

"What if the closet gets too hot?"

"I'm right here. I'll keep checking it."

"All night? That's what we really should do, y'know. We ought to see how he is every few minutes. Remember how Dad peeled? You don't want that to happen to him, do you?"

He did have a point. "Okay," I said, sliding over to one side of my bed. "But the pillow is *mine* and so is one-half of the bed, so stay on *your* side."

"All right, Stingy," he said, getting under the covers and spreading out over ninety-nine percent of my bed.

The whole warm wonderful feeling of Christmas was gone as soon as I felt one of his cold feet on my leg. After that, even the lights, which had looked so pretty before, started to annoy me. But the thing that really got on my nerves was the "Unka Rogie" business.

Five seconds wouldn't go by without him hopping

out of bed to run over to the closet to see how things were. Then he'd get back in, and just when I'd get used to his cold feet and my measly one percent of the bed, he'd throw off the covers and charge back to the closet again.

"You okay, Pweshus? Des tell Unka Rogie here."

"Hi. It's Unka Rogie peekin' in to see if you's still comfy."

"Awww, how's da sunny-wunny lampy doin'? Des tell Unka Rogie."

I swear those were his exact words, and for the life of me I don't know how Wally could stand them. I sure couldn't and the next time he went in I covered my head with my pillow, but I heard him anyway.

"You des wait till you see what Unka Rogie's makin' for da pweshus in his math class. A desert diorama . . . dat's what he's makin'."

Actually, I think I could've put up with the lights and the closet checks, maybe even all the Unka Rogie's . . . *if* I hadn't been pushed right over the edge of my bed.

"Look," I said, picking myself up off the floor, "one more time and you're going back to your room. Understand?"

"All right," he said, "I won't do it again."

I got under the covers and shoved him over to his side. "Lay straight on your back with your arms folded across your chest and your feet together, like I'm doing."

He sat up and looked at me. "Like a mummy?"

"Right. And another thing. One closet check every twenty minutes. No more."

I guess he believed what I'd said about going back to his room, because he got so quiet it started worrying me. "It's all right to breathe," I said.

"Thanks," he gasped.

I was so wide awake I knew I'd never fall asleep. Or even doze, for that matter. I'd started listening to sounds that hadn't bothered me in years, like the wind tapping a trellis against the side of the house and a branch of the black walnut tree scraping across my screen.

But those were nothing compared to the sounds inside the house. Like fifty-year-old floors that still think they've got to settle down every night, a faucet dripping in the bathroom sink, *and* Wally coming to life in the closet.

I could hear him scratching around on his newspapers and I figured he thought it was daylight since he had the sun-lamp on.

"You asleep?" I asked Rog.

"One of my arms is," he said. "Why? Is it time to go check?"

"Nope. Another twelve minutes. I was just wondering . . . since the box is yours . . . how'd you like to clean it first?"

8
The Miracle

I did learn a couple of very important lessons Friday night. One was that I'd never share a bed with Roger again unless my life depended on it. The other was that our heating system for Wally was crummy . . . horrible-crummy. Something had to be done about it. Either that, or I could forget about sleep for the next few weeks.

"Hey, Price, you're about as speedy as a radish," Skeeter said, when we were playing ball the next afternoon. "Anything wrong?"

I could've made up an excuse like my arm was hurting, but he seemed to know that Wally had something to do with the way I was feeling. "Problems with the dinosaur?"

"Yeah," I said. Then I told him everything.

"Boy, Price, no wonder you clammed up on the bus yesterday morning. Between Snag and your mother, and no sleep, you're worse off than I am."

Instead of playing any more ball, we sat in the park racking our brains to think of something that could be done to improve S.L.S.T. "Well, there's only one thing you can do," he said, digging in his jeans pocket. "Buy one of those heating lights that Billy uses." He put some change in my hand. "My allowance. C'mon now, keep it! I'll mooch comics and candy off kids at school next week."

"Thanks, Skeet, I . . ."

"Aw, forget it. You'd do the same thing for me . . . I know you would."

When I got home, Rog and I pooled all the money we had between us. It came to nine dollars and forty-seven cents, including Skeeter's allowance and the three quarters we were able to shake out of Snag's piggy bank. After we counted it, I called a pet store.

"You the Wiggins' kid?" the man at the store asked when I told him what I needed.

"No," I said, "I'm a friend of the Wiggins' kid."

"Just asking . . . the Wiggins' kid is usually the only customer I've got for Vita-Lites. I always keep a few on hand just for him."

"Do you have a cheap one?" I asked.

"Got one for about nine dollars. That's the smallest size."

"Great," I said, stuffing all of the money into my wallet. "That's the size I wanted. Could you hold it for me? I'll be in as soon as I can."

"Sure thing, and what about a fixture to go along with it? Or do you already have one?"

"Fixture? What fixture?" I asked. "Don't the lights plug in by themselves?"

"No-siree, you've got to mount them in special attachments . . . fixtures. They'll run you about forty-five dollars including the thermostat. Want me to set one of them aside for you too?"

"No thanks," I said, dumping the money back out of my wallet. "And I guess I won't be coming in after all."

After I'd hung up, Rog and I did the next best thing we could do. We moved the sun-lamp almost up to the ceiling and adjusted it so it wouldn't glare right into the box. Then we hauled a third rock up from the rock garden and laid it on top of the other two rocks so it formed a sort of bridge that Wally could crawl under if he got too hot.

Even so, an hour of sun-lamp time was as much as we thought it was safe to give him in one dose. And that meant an hour every *other* hour.

It took me most of Saturday to work out a very complicated switch-on-off-again time schedule, but I had it ready by bedtime. Starting that night, I had to stay awake till 11:00, turn on the sun-lamp, then set my alarm for 1:00 before I went to sleep.

Rog, on the other hand, was able to go to bed any old time he wanted, just as long as he first set his alarm for 12:00. When it went off, he had to come into my room and pull out the plug that I'd stayed up till 11:00 to plug in . . . but before he could go back to bed, he had to re-set his alarm for 2:00. This was so he could get up to pull out the plug that I'd gotten up at 1:00 to plug in. But it didn't end there. I still had to get up at 3:00 and 5:00 to plug in . . . and Roger still had to get up at 4:00 and 6:00 to pull out.

I suppose if I'd looked at the advantages from Wally's point of view, I might have thought it was *the* perfect system. But I didn't look at it from Wally's point of view. I looked at it from mine. And as far as I was concerned, it was still horrible . . . crummy. But just not as horrible-crummy as zero sleep.

Roger didn't seem to mind it as much as I did. By the third night he was such a pro at finding his way around in the dark that he knew the exact number of steps it took to get from his alarm clock to my closet.

"Want to hear something neato?" he asked, practically shaking my arm off to wake me up during one of his four-o'clock tours. "If I start counting the minute I get out of bed . . . by the time I reach seventeen I'm standing in front of the plug. Seventeen steps! Isn't that wild?"

"Wild," I repeated.

"And d'ya know what else? A few more times and I'll

be able to come in here without feeling along the walls with my hands . . . or bumping into anything."

He was right about finally being able to make it to my closet without his hands. The only thing was, it took him fifty-three steps. And he did bump into something on the way. Snaggletooth. Heading for the bathroom.

"Ohhh, no you don't," she yelled when she realized who'd crashed into her. "I needed to go in there before you did and you're just gonna have to wait till I come out."

Roger didn't say a word. Not even when she flicked on a hall light. He closed his eyes and held his arms out in front of him like he was walking in his sleep; then he circled the hallway a couple of times until she stopped staring at him and went into the bathroom. As soon as the door closed behind her, he hurried into my closet and pulled out the plug.

He woke me up to tell me about it. The next day Snag told everybody else. She told every kid on the bus. She told the bus driver. She told every kid she saw on the playground. She even told her whole class for Show and Tell, and gave them a demonstration of how Roger walked with his eyes closed and his arms out in front of him.

The thing that really got me about our switch-on-switch-off operation was that Roger wasn't even looking tired from it. When he got up for good each morning, no one ever would've guessed he'd made all those round trips traipsing back and forth between our rooms at night.

Wally still didn't appreciate what *I* was going through for him. At the end of the first week he wasn't any more my "Old Buddy" than Marvin Oates was. The Peach Delight hadn't done a bit of good and neither had all the desserts I'd sacrificed so I could give him fruit. He didn't even care that I'd had a turn changing his newspapers. Besides, I was beginning to look worn out.

"Are you feeling all right, Michael?" Mom asked one day.

"Fine," I said, trying to hold my head up and not yawn while she felt my forehead.

"You don't look fine to me. You've got dark circles under your eyes and seem to be exhausted lately. I think you should have a check-up."

A check-up might not be so bad from a doctor who thumps your chest and looks at your eyelids. But our doctor goes all out with blood tests and little see-through containers you have to put your name on and leave with his nurse.

I made up my mind that no one was dragging me over to see him, and I told Mom that the only thing wrong with me was the trellis.

"The trellis?" she asked.

"Yeah. It keeps pounding on the house at night and I can't sleep."

She promised me she'd fix the trellis herself, right away. Then I made a promise. To me. And it was to come up with a mighty fast solution for replacing the system Rog and I were using.

Only what, I wondered.

The idea came when I happened to walk by the rusty thermometer that's nailed to the outside of our garage. I decided to borrow it for a while.

Wally needed around ninety to ninety-five degrees to keep happy and healthy, and I began experimenting with different lightbulbs in my desk lamp. By bending down the stem so it was about six inches above the thermometer, it took me just half an afternoon to figure out that a hundred-watt bulb only raised the mercury a few degrees. Next, I tried a hundred-and-fifty-watt bulb, and the day I was recording the heat it gave, I noticed something in our backyard. Mom's prize Talisman roses had started blooming.

The last thing Billy'd told me when I walked off with Wally was to give him some of Mom's roses, and since the book said chuckwallas loved yellow, I was sure I'd hit on a winner. I figured it wouldn't even matter that they had a little orange around the edges. They're still yellow, I thought, and they're still roses.

What's more, I couldn't have noticed them at a better time. Snag had packed up her dolls to play with her friend Amy down the block, and Mom was at the hardware store getting some wire and nails to fix the trellis.

The only one hanging around the house was Roger, and I knew it wasn't going to be long till I got rid of him. He'd made plans to go bike riding with a bunch of kids in the neighborhood, which was perfect, because I had no intention of ever telling him about the roses. He didn't need anything extra to butter up Wally.

As soon as he'd left, I started stripping off some of the outer petals and putting them in a plastic bag. I didn't dare pick a *whole* Talisman. Mom has such a thing about them that I wouldn't have put it past her to have counted every last one.

When the bag was full, I tried the same method Rog used with fruit to coat the petals with vitamins: just pour a little powder in . . . and shake. Then I hid the bag in my desk to save until bedtime. And that night, for the first time since Wally had been staying with us, I didn't ask for fruit for dessert. I had a great big piece of chocolate cake with fudge frosting . . . and it was delicious.

"Boy, are *you* selfish," Rog said to me later. "How could you do that? You want him to starve?"

"We were wasting fruit, Roger. Besides, look at his tail. At least a week's fat is stored in it."

Roger was so mad he didn't care about Wally's fat and before he left he gave him some Shake 'n Bake grapes and told him how awful I was. "Neber you mind, Pweshus. Maybe rotten old Unka Mikey doesn't think 'bout you, but Unka Rogie do."

When Rog left, I got the bag of petals out of my desk drawer and glanced at the thermometer. It read eighty-eight degrees, which meant I was getting so close to target that a two-hundred watter would probably do the job.

This is it, I thought, going into the closet. No more S.L.S.T.

Then I knelt down in front of the box and held out some of the petals. "Remember me, Wally . . . the guy you hate? Well, in case you're interested, I've got something yellow for you."

I don't know whether it was what I said that got to him, or whether he just smelled the Talismans, but all of a sudden the miracle of miracles happened . . . *Wally actually came over to me!*

He didn't go overboard and leap into my arms and give me a kiss or anything. He just strolled out from under his bridge, blinked a couple of times, and walked over to my hand. Then he ate a petal. Then another. And by the time he'd had four, I picked him up. V e r y gently and v e r y slowly.

Roger was right about his belly. It was hot. And his skin really was soft. Maybe not silky . . . but soft. And he did look like he was sort of smiling. "Well, now," I said, holding him up to my face so I could get a closer look at him. "Did da widdle pweshus like da pwitty yellow floweys?"

9
The Big Scare

Roger didn't believe me when I told him about the two-hundred-watt bulb.

"I know *you*," he said, after I'd moved the desk lamp next to the box. "You're just trying to get out of getting up at night, that's what you're trying to do . . . but *I'm* gonna keep coming in here."

And he did. . . even though I'd taped the thermometer onto one of the rocks to convince him that two-hundred watts gave a steady ninety-three degrees. He didn't believe the thermometer any more than he believed me, however, so four times a night I *still* had to listen to him asking Wally if he was warm enough.

The only good thing I had going for me were the Talismans. Every day I brought Wally a bag of petals before I went to bed, and it wasn't long before Mom started concentrating on something besides the circles under my eyes.

"I can't understand what's happening to my roses this year," she complained one day while she was pruning and weeding. "They're so skimpy."

They were, but it seemed like a small price to pay for the way Wally looked when he ate them. He was crazy about Talismans, and after a while he was completely ignoring Roger's fruit.

"See that?" Rog asked me one night. "He's going to you. . . and d'ya know why? Cuz he's wondering how come you're not feeding him anymore."

"That's not the reason," I said.

"Oh, yeah? What is the reason, then?"

"It's a secret, Rog. . . but I'll tell you if you promise me something."

"What?" he asked.

"You have to promise me you'll stop coming in here at night."

Rog didn't aswer right away, but when Wally nuzzled up to me like I was his favorite person, Rog couldn't stand it any longer. "Okay. I won't come in. Tell me."

"Uh-uh," I said. "Not till I see if you can keep you word."

I wasn't sure whether he could go through a night without making his rounds to see if Wally was "comfy," but he'll do almost anything to find out a secret. Finally I told him about the Talismans.

"But don't go ape," I warned, "Mom's already onto something."

Two days after Rog started in on the petals, Mom stormed into the kitchen during breakfast. "Just look at these," she said, throwing a handful of stripped Talismans on the table. "There's hardly anything left to them."

Dad put down his coffee cup and Rog and I sat quieter than mice while Snag picked up one of the remains and twirled it around in her fingers. "That's not true, Mom. See? You've still got the centers."

Mom slammed her fist down so hard on the table our cereal bowls bounced. *"Three days* until the flower show. . . and what've I got? *Centers!"*

"Boy, doesn't time fly," I said, taking a bite out of my toast. "Seems like we just had the last flower show . . . and here it is again. . . "

"Right. . . Sunday afternoon," she roared, scooping up the flowers and waving them in the air. "And *these* are what everybody's coming to see." We watched her hurl the flowers into the garbage, then she clomped out of the room ranting about how she couldn't *wait* to get her hands on whatever it was that was attacking her Talismans.

"I hope none of you had anything to do with this," Dad said after she'd gone.

"Who. . . *us?"* squeaked Rog. "I'll bet the mole did it."

Snag dropped another marshmallow into her hot

chocolate, then shrugged. "I don't know what the big fuss is about. Mom's got lots of other flowers. Maybe something else'll win for a change."

That afternoon, Mom canceled out of the flower show, and for the next three days she was about as pleasant as a rattlesnake. Rog and I tiptoed around the house, doing everything we could to avoid her, but mostly we stuck to my room guarding the closet.

"Shorry, Pweshus," Rog apologized to Wally when we switched him back to a fruit diet, "but dere's a mean lady watchin'da pwitty floweys."

Neither of us could wait until the weekend was over, but by dinnertime on Saturday we thought Mom looked like she was calming down a bit. We were wrong. "I've got an announcement to make," she said, slapping a half-frozen pizza on the table. "I'm taking up pottery again."

Rog was as relieved as I was, but Snag was more interested in what was sitting in the middle of the table. "Hey," she said, sticking her fork into a solid clump of cheese, "how're we supposed to eat this. . . it's still got ice in it."

"Eat it anyway," Mom snapped. "That's all I'm fixing."

While Dad was reheating the pizza, he asked us if we had any suggestions about things we could do to get away from the house on Sunday. Mom wasn't exactly jumping for joy over anything that was mentioned, but when the list boiled down to bowling, a picnic in the canyon, or going to a carwash, she finally agreed to go on a picnic.

We got a very early start the next morning since Snag can't sleep past sunrise when she's excited about going somewhere. "Come on, rise and shine," she yelled, pounding on everybody's door at 6:00 A.M. "We want to get out of the house today. . . remember?"

No matter how much we dragged out breakfast or took our time packing the picnic basket, we were still ready to leave by 8:30. Mom was the last one in the car, and I knew right away that she wasn't in any mood for jokes.

"Nice sweatshirt you've got on, Mom," Rog told her when we were driving out of town. "Isn't that the one you wear when you're weeding?"

Mom glared at him from behind her dark glasses, and then there was this terrible silence that lasted till we got up to the canyon. After that nobody breathed a word about anything that was the teeniest bit connected with flowers. Even the word "trees" seemed too close, so we called them "those tall things."

Mom might've forgotten the flower show altogether, if our whole block hadn't been lined with cars when we drove back.

"Would you look at *that?*" Snag hollered when we pulled into the driveway. "Somebody must be having an outdoor party."

"In our yard?" Roger asked.

Mom stared out the window and groaned as she watched hordes of people milling around her flower beds. "I can't understand it. . . I just can't understand it," she kept repeating. "I distinctly told Doris Greenberg I was canceling."

Dad turned off the ignition and looked at her. "Maybe Doris thought you were talking about the Talismans. There must have been some kind of mix-up . . . because everybody's out there."

"You can say that again," said Rog. "Every garden freak in town."

At first Mom refused to get out of the car, but the lady who works in the donut shop spotted us and Mom had to wave back. Finally we all piled out, and Doris Greenberg, who's always re-elected President of the Garden Club every year, came running over.

"Here comes The Empress," Rog whispered.

"I've got good news for you, Catherine," Mrs. Greenberg said to Mom. "I think you're going to take first place with your Spitfire gladiolas."

"My what. . . *Spitfires?*"

"Yes, isn't that wonderful?"

"C'mom, let's get our skateboards," I said to Rog. "Maybe Skeeter and Josh can come with us.

He started following me, and when we were almost to the garage we saw Snag weaving her way through the crowds to get over to the group that was huddled around the Talismans. "Anybody want to see what ate Mom's roses?" she blurted out.

As soon as he heard that, Rog wanted to dash upstairs and block my door. "Wait, "I said, grabbing his sleeve. "Maybe nobody'll pay any attention to her."

The words were barely out of my mouth when a circle of heads turned to Snag. "You know what it was?" a voice asked.

"Yeah," she said. "If you wanna follow me, I'll show you where it's hiding."

"Ooohh, nooo," Rog started screeching. "Michael, look who's coming with her!"

It was hard to believe at first, but Old Snaggletooth was leading half of the neighborhood across the lawn. And the worst part was, she was grinning from ear to ear.

"I'll go shove a chair in front of your door. . . and you try to stop them," Rog told me as he took off for the house. "Thow up, tackle them, have a sunstroke . . . *anything!"*

I was preparing myself for the sunstroke when Snag suddenly came to a halt. "There," she said, pointing to the ground. "We have a mole. . . and it's right in that burrow there."

Roger had already made it to the house, so I took off after him and we ended up watching the rest of the flower show from my room.

"Does da widdle pweshus wanna see da lady who

growed all da yummy yellow floweys?" Rog asked Wally as he carried him over to the window. "Dere she is . . . da one in da baggy sweatshirt."

"Just make sure the lady in the baggy sweatshirt doesn't look up here and see what ate her yummy yellow flowers," I told him.

"She won't. She's too busy yacking away with The Empress. Just look at her."

I stopped watching Snag give a lady with a donut hairdo a guided tour to the burrow and glanced across the yard at Mom. "She looks awful."

"Besides that. Do you notice anything different about her? See. . . she's doing it right now. Everytime The Empress says something to her. . . she smiles."

"Maybe the blue ribbon's a sure thing."

"You wouldn't suppose they rigged it, would you?"

"Naw, what's in it for Mrs. Greenberg? She doesn't need Mom's vote. She's elected every year anyhow."

"Maybe so," he said, "but I still think they're cooking something up."

10
The Rotten Good News

Mom surprised us all. Instead of going back to her old grouchy self after the flower show was over, she practically became human again.

To me, it was obvious that the blue ribbon for the Spitfires was the reason behind her sudden recovery. So I was nearly bowled over a couple of nights later when I found out the *real* reason.

"Your mother and I have some very good news for the three of you," Dad announced as they waltzed into the den. Then he turned off the TV and they stood smiling and holding hands like they were getting ready for a press conference.

"Ohhh, nooo," Rog groaned. "Not Aunt Florence. Is *she* coming again?"

"In August," said Mom.

"Is *that* the good news?" I asked.

"No, dear. Something else. The Greenbergs are moving to Florida . . ."

"What d'ya know," Rog cut in, giving me a poke. "Didn't I tell you they were cooking up something?" I shrugged and he turned back to Mom. "Go ahead . . . break it to us. Now *you're* going to be the new Empress . . . right?"

"Wrong. I wouldn't have that job for anything, and I wish you'd stop interrupting me. Now where was I?"

"The Greenbergs," I said.

"Oh, yes. The Greenbergs. Well, it's as simple as this . . . they're moving and we're thinking about buying their house."

"What d'ya mean, we're thinking about buying their house?" Rog yelled. "I haven't thought a *thing* about it!"

"And neither have I," Snag pitched in, "and what's more, I'm not going to. So you can just turn that TV right back on."

Usually a bossy comment like that doesn't go over so well, but Mom and Dad let it go by without batting an eyelash. "Susan," Dad said, in his try-to-be-patient voice, "why don't you give us a chance to tell you about the house? If you do . . . you'll change your mind."

"HA!"

For a minute I thought the fireworks were going to start popping, but Dad took a deep breath and shifted his attention to Rog and me. "As far as you boys are concerned . . . just think . . . you won't have to complain about a partition anymore. You'll have your own separate rooms."

"Who's complaining?" I asked. "I like the partition . . . it's sort of like having an intercom. I can ask Rog something and he can answer me and we don't even have to bother going over on each other's side."

"Well, that settles it," Snag said. "They like their partition, and I don't have one, anyway . . . so we don't have to move."

"It's going to be a wonderful change for all of us," Mom said, pulling up a chair and sitting down. "For one thing, the house is almost new, so we won't have problems with the pipes, and none of you will have to listen to the floors creaking."

"No more floors creaking," Rog hollered. "I *happen* to *love* creaking floors."

"Keep your voice down, dear."

"Well, I do. I'm *crazy* about them."

"How can you say that, Roger? You're the one who used to have me up every night, because you thought there were ghosts walking around." Mom slumped down in her chair and stared up at the ceiling. "It's your turn, Harold. See if you can tell them anything."

"All right," Dad said. "How about the garage?"

"The garage?" Rog jumped off the couch so he was facing me. "What's the matter with these people?" he

screamed. "Don't they know we've already *got* a garage?"

"ROGER! SIT DOWN!"

"But we do, Dad. It's right out in back."

"It's a *one*-car garage. The Greenbergs have a *two*-car garage."

"But we've only got *one* car . . . count it."

"I don't need to count it, because I know we've got three bicycles, garden tools, basketballs, fishing rods, and a thousand and one *other* things we can store in the empty side. Anyway . . . that's not what I wanted to tell you. The important thing is what's over their garage."

"What?" I asked. "A roof?"

"A studio. A huge studio workshop . . . where you can paint, use clay, make puppets, or anything you want. Your mother's going to do her pottery up there, and we'll have plenty of room for all the projects we've been dying to do for years." Dad paused for a minute, and I'm sure he was secretly thinking he'd pulled the fastest con-job on earth over on us. "In fact," he continued, using his con-job smile, "if we find a buyer for this house right away, we might be in there by the middle of the summer. That should give you a chance to do some of those projects before your new school starts."

The three of us looked at each other. *"New school?"*

"That's right. You'll all be going to Orchard."

"Not me," said Rog. "I'm not going there for anything. I know what that principal does . . . he beats kids!"

"That's sheer nonsense," Dad snapped. "Arnold Oates is an excellent superintendent. He'd never allow anything like that to go on in one of his schools."

"Then why does he send Marvin to Pine Ridge?" I asked. "Just think about that while we're all on the subject."

We must've argued for another hour, but Mom and Dad didn't give two hoots about the way we felt. And it didn't seem to make a dent that none of us cared about the copper pipes, the dumb old studio, or the extra bathroom.

What we did care about was democracy. But good old-fashioned, down-to-earth democracy doesn't exist in our family, because our family is controlled by dictators. Dad made that perfectly clear after we'd all voted on the Greenberg house.

"Your mother and I know it'll take a while for the three of you to get used to the idea of moving," he said, brushing aside the fact that the votes *against* it were three out of five. "But keep this in mind: we're doing it for you."

As soon as I heard that, I decided I'd had enough for one night, and I told everybody I was going to bed. "Wait a minute, dear," Mom said, stopping me. "Our house is going on the market in a few days and I want you to know that ahead of time, so you won't be surprised when you find people going through your room."

"Can't you just *tell* them what it looks like?"

"Of course not, Michael. They're going to want to see it for themselves. But that shouldn't be a problem. You've been keeping your room in great shape lately. Even your closet . . . I haven't had to hang up your clothes in days." With that she gave me a hug and kissed me good night.

"Susan! Roger! Back in here," Dad called as they both tried sneaking out behind me. "We're going to have a nice chat about the pigpens the two of you live in."

I hurried upstairs and when I got to my room I took out the bag of Talisman petals I'd started collecting after the show and brought them to Wally. "Dere ya go, Pweshus," I told him as he nibbled one out of my hand. "Eat all the floweys you want cuz it doesn't matter . . . nothing matters around here anymore."

As rotten as I was feeling, it made me feel a lot better just watching him. "Come on," I said when he was finished, "Unka Mikey's gonna let da widdle guy do his favorite trick." Wally climbed into my hand and I carried him over to my desk and pulled out the drawers for him. "Dere ya go . . . funsy-time."

Just then Rog came steaming in and slammed the door. "It's a dirty trick," he said, plunking himself down on my bed. "What do they think we are . . . gypsies? I'm telling you, Michael, if we let them get away with it this time, the next thing you know, they're gonna try it again. With a *three*-car garage."

"I don't think there are any," I said. "But you're right. They'll come up with something."

"What d'ya think we ought to do . . . run away?"

"Where? To Pittsburgh . . . so we can live with Aunt Florence?"

He didn't say anything, and we both sat mulling things over while Wally burrowed through the stack of papers I'd saved when I worked out our switch-on-switch-off-again schedule.

"You know what I'll miss?" Rog asked finally.

"What? The tire swing," I said, thinking about the afternoon we'd all watched Dad put it up in the walnut tree.

"That too. But there's something I'm gonna miss even more. The banister."

I looked at him. "How do you know the Greenbergs don't have one?"

"To heck with the Greenbergs. I'm used to this one. I can get downstairs in two and a half seconds when I use it. Besides," he sighed, "I love this house, I love our neighborhood, I love our yard, I love all the kids who live around here, I love. . ."

"Marvin Oates?"

"Well . . . except for him, I love everybody. Don't you?"

I nodded. "Especially Billy and Skeeter. Life just isn't going to be the same without them."

"Or Wally," he said, burying his head in his hands.

"We'll probably never get a chance to visit him once he's back at the greenhouse. And I just don't think I could stand it, Michael, if he forgot about us."

"Why don't we talk about something else?"

"Okay. But do you think he will?"

"I said I don't want to talk about it."

Rog got up and paced around the room for a while. "I just thought of something," he said, chewing on a hangnail. "Do you remember how Florida sticks way out in the water when you look at it on a map?"

"Yeah, and if you think it's going to break off and float away before the Greenbergs move there . . . forget it."

"How'd you know what I was gonna say?"

"I know how you think, Roger."

"Well, it *is* possible. Anything's possible, y'know. What do you think the chances are?"

"Not good," I said.

He plunked himself back down on the bed, and we went through a hundred or more other possibilities until we were so tired we could hardly keep our eyes open. "Keep thinking," he said with a yawn. "And we'll talk some more when we're on the bus in the morning."

After he went to his room I took off my clothes and just left them in a heap on the floor. Then I got into bed and fell asleep without realizing I had my socks on. Unfortunately, taking my socks off wasn't all I forgot to do. . . .

11
"P.S. How's Wally?"

*I*t's hard to believe that something two feet long can up and disappear overnight, but that's exactly what Wally did.

The mess was there . . . no doubt about that. Papers were scattered all over the top of my desk, the drawers were still sticking out, and my calendar was knocked over along with my can of pencils and the plastic skeleton Skeeter had given me for my birthday. As soon as I'd opened my eyes, I saw them . . . and then it hit me. I'd forgotten to put Wally back in his box.

I flew out of bed hoping I'd find him sleeping somewhere under the papers, but he wasn't. And he wasn't in any of the bottom drawers either. I dumped them out after I'd scouted through the papers, and once I had, it didn't take me long to realize he was nowhere in, on, or under my desk.

So I started looking in, on, and under everything else: my bed, wastepaper basket, rock collection, shell collection, miscellaneous collection, yesterday's clothes collection, bookshelves . . . and finally the closet . . . praying he'd had the sense to go back in there. But he hadn't.

At that point I was only *half* scared out of my wits. I wasn't completely scared out of them, because the door had been closed all night. Wally had to be somewhere in my room. Only where, I wondered, after I'd combed through every inch of it.

"Boy, oh, boy, are you gonna look funny going to school in your socks and shorts," Rog said, when he came in.

"Quick . . . close the door," I yelled. "And keep it closed."

Then I told him.

No one would believe his hysteria. The screaming and the shouting were sort of ordinary, but the tantrum on the floor, the total ransacking of my room till it looked like the background for one of those World War II movies and the accusations weren't. They weren't anywhere near ordinary. They were unreal.

When he went down for breakfast, Mom and Dad were sure he was crying his eyes out because he didn't want to move or go to Orchard. Rog always cries and eats when he's upset. Not me. I don't cry anymore, and I can't stand the sight of food, which was part of the reason why I wasn't having breakfast.

The other part was because I was too busy searching under all of the rubble. "Michael," Mom shouted as she stomped up the stairs, "just what is this business about you and Roger staying home today?" Then she opened my door and got a good look at the World War II number.

"I can explain," I said, throwing my blankets and pillow onto my bed and trying to think of something fast.

"EXPLAIN? Let *me* explain something. If you don't get this place cleaned up the moment you get home from school . . ."

"But . . ."

"Don't 'but' me! You're going to school, and this house is *still* going on the market . . . no matter what kind of stunt you pull. *Furthermore, I'm not picking up one thing! Nothing! I'm not setting foot inside this room all day!*"

There were lots of threats to speed us up, but it still took a while for Rog and me to get in any kind of condition for school. By the time we were ready, the bus was long gone with Snaggletooth on board, so Dad volunteered to drive us on his way to work.

"You haven't even *seen* the Greenbergs' house yet," he told us as the car screeched down the block. "So it's

absolutely ridiculous the way you're carrying on . . .
and Roger, *stop* crying!"

The speeches and the wailing went on and on, but I
sort of tuned them out and just kept my mouth shut till
we pulled up in front of the school.

" . . . and no more sabotage," Dad said, kicking us
out of the car. "I want *positive* thinking."

The only positive thing I could think of the rest of
the day was that my door was closed and Mom wasn't
going to set foot in my room. Other than that, I spent
my time worrying about Wally.

"Hey, Price," Skeeter whispered as he slid into the
seat next to me during lunch. "Everytime I went in the
boys' room this morning, Roger-Dodger was in there
crying. Anything happen to the dinosaur?"

"He's lost," I said, looking around to make sure no
one else was listening. "But that's only *half* of the
story."

"This isn't your month, Price," Skeeter told me after he'd heard about Wally *and* the Greenbergs' house.

He offered to come over and help search for Wally
when school was out, but I had to turn him down. "It's
not safe," I explained. "Wait till the reptile-hater's in a
better mood."

Going home he saved seats for Rog and me at the
back of the bus. We didn't say much, and when we
stopped at our corner, he gave each of us a pat on the
shoulder. "Good luck, guys."

"Better hurry, Michael," Snag called as she hopped off. "Someone's standing on the front steps waiting for you."

It was Mom. "NOT ONE BLESSED THING TO EAT UNTIL THAT ROOM IS STRAIGHTENED," she thundered when I came up the steps and walked past her. She wasn't half as rotten to Snag and Rog and told them there were some cookies on the kitchen counter.

"Later," Rog said, following me inside. "I want to help Michael, first."

I raced ahead till I got to the upstairs hall and saw that my door was halfway open. "Hey," I shouted down to Mom, "I thought you weren't going to set foot in my room."

"I didn't. I just opened your door so I could toss your postcard inside."

"What postcard?"

"YOU FIND IT!"

Rog and I squeezed in, as far as we could go, then closed the door. "Now don't go to pieces," I told him. "Wally couldn't possibly have gotten past the mess you made . . . *we* can't even wade through it."

Both of us zipped through things, picking up here . . . putting away there, turning whatever was upside down right side up, and looking for Wally and the post-card at the same time.

When everything was almost straightened, we

found the card. . . . It was from the *last* person I wanted to think about. Billy Wiggins.

"What does he have to say?" Rog asked, starting to cry all over again.

I looked at the picture of an Indian woman weaving a basket, and a bunch of sheep grazing off in the background. Then I turned it over.

"GREETINGS FROM ARIZONA," it began. "HAVING A NIFTY VACATION. WILL BE BACK HOME ON JUNE 3, THEN THERE'S ONLY ONE MORE WEEK OF SCHOOL BEFORE SUMMER VACATION."

"Oh, great!" Rog said, wiping his eyes and his nose with the back of his hand. "Doesn't he ever have anything but vacations?" Then he nudged me. "Well . . . go on!"

"VISITED SOME TERRIFIC RESERVATIONS AND BOUGHT YOU A HANDMADE SURPRISE ON ONE OF THEM. THE PICTURE IS A HINT. YOUR PAL, B.W.

"P.S. HOW'S WALLY?"

Rog sniffed. *"He* would have to ask that." Then he took the card and looked at the picture. "What d'ya think he's bringing you . . . a basket?"

"Either that or some sheep," I answered. "But we'll worry about that later. Right now we're going to get some Talismans so Wally'll come out of hiding."

"But Mom's downstairs. She'll see us."

"All right," I said. "You go down and keep her and Snag company while you feed your face with cookies, and I'll get them."

I didn't just get what was left of the Talismans. I stripped the petals off anything that was yellow and smelled good, and when Rog came back upstairs we put little piles of them in different parts of my room. "There," I said, when we were finished, "that ought to do it."

We sat on the floor, and waited. And waited. And waited. Till dinnertime.

"He's got to come out while we're eating," I told Rog when Mom called us.

But he didn't.

Or after dinner. We knew *that* as soon as we checked every petal in every pile. There wasn't so much as a crunch mark. Nothing.

"Poor little lost Wally," Rog told me at bedtime. "He's gonna starve."

"The book says he can go for days without eating."

"But he must be hungry, Michael."

"Then he'll come out," I said. "You'll see, he'll come out while we're sleeping."

Rog scattered some more petals over my rug like confetti. "Please," he begged, "let me stay in here and wait. I won't say a word. I promise."

"In your own room," I said, pushing him out the door. "I'll let you know the minute he comes out of hiding."

12
The Bad Dream

I'm not sure how long I'd been asleep when I heard it, but it woke me up. One of Snag's screams could jar somebody right out of a coma.

"What's going on?" I asked Roger when we poked our heads out of our doors at the same time.

"You got me," he whispered. "But I think Mom and Dad ran in there."

The door was open to Snag's room and we saw a light go on. "I WAS NOT HAVING A NIGHTMARE," she yelled. "IT WAS A MONSTER! AND I SAW IT . . . AND IT WALKED RIGHT ACROSS MY BED."

Rog glared at me. "I thought you said he couldn't *possibly* wade through your room."

"Look," I said, "it's no time to pick a fight. Let's see what happened."

We tiptoed down the hall together and peeked in her room. Snag was standing on top of her pillow at the corner of her bed, and Mom and Dad were trying to talk her into getting back down. "IT WAS THIS BIG," she shouted, stretching her hands wide apart, "AND IT SORT OF SAT ON MY LEG . . . BLINKING AT ME."

"Susan," Mom said, "I know dreams can seem very real sometimes, but . . ."

"HOW MANY TIMES DO I HAVE TO TELL YOU? IT WASN'T A DREAM . . . I SAW IT AND IT LOOKED LIKE A DRAGON."

Dad sat on the foot of her bed. "Susan, this is going to seem so silly to you tomorrow. You know there's no such thing as a dragon."

"HA!"

"I used to dream about monsters and dragons all the time," said Roger. The three of them turned their heads and saw us standing in the doorway. "Well . . . I did."

"So did I," I added. "Practically every night when my second teeth were coming in. That's what causes them y'know."

Rog nodded. "That's right. I'll bet it's her crooked one that's doing this."

"LIARS."

"I don't like that word," Mom snapped.

99

"WELL, THEY ARE. AND I'M NOT COMING DOWN OFF THIS PILLOW TILL SOMEBODY GETS THAT MONSTER OUT OF HERE."

Dad stood up. "If it'll make you feel better, I'll go through your entire room looking for it. But you've got to promise me you'll settle down afterwards."

"NOT TILL YOU TRAP IT."

Just then, Rog and I saw a tail streak under her dresser. "WAIT," cried Rog, as he ran over to her bed. "I know what you saw . . . one of *these!*"

Snag looked at where he was pointing on her bedspread. "That's a *daisy,* you *dumbhead.*"

"But it could look like a monster in the dark. Tell her, Dad."

"This is getting out of hand," Mom sighed.

"Yes, it certainly is." Dad glanced at his watch. "It's almost 3:30, and I've got to be in the office early in the morning."

"I have an idea," I said. "I'm not afraid to sleep in here, so why don't we switch and she can sleep in my room?" Then I remembered the petals all over my rug. "Nope . . . I take that back. Make it Roger's room."

"Great idea. I'll sleep in here," he said.

"We'll both sleep in here."

"How about it?" Dad yawned.

"Fine with me," said Snag, climbing down from her pillow and grinning to beat the band. "I can't wait to see if it eats them up."

As soon as Mom and Dad took her into Rog's room, I

closed the door and looked under her dresser. "He's gone. Did you see him go anywhere?"

Rog shook his head and made a dive under Snag's bed. "He's not under here, either."

"Well, he's somewhere," I whispered. "He couldn't possibly have gotten out of here."

"That's what you said before."

"But he couldn't have. Wanna take a look in her closet and I'll check her desk?"

"Could you please tell me why this light is still on?" Dad asked, opening the door. "And Roger, what're you doing in Susan's closet . . . you're not really looking for a monster, are you?"

"Uh-uh. I was just trying to find . . . um . . ."

"The button that fell off his pajamas," I finished.

"Well, you can look for it tomorrow. Now get some sleep . . . both of you."

"Is that all, Dad?" I asked as I practically shut the door in his face.

"No . . . actually it isn't," he said, pushing the door open again. "You boys disappeared after dinner so you didn't hear who's coming over tomorrow."

"Who?" I asked.

"Some people to see the house . . . and you'd better behave." He closed the door, then gave it a rap. "Get that light off."

Rog turned it off and we started searching around in the dark. "I don't know how she saw him. I can hardly see anything. Can you?"

"Not much."

"Think we ought to get in her bed and wait? Maybe he'll walk across it again."

"You get in," I said, feeling around on top of her desk. "Ahhh . . . here we go."

"Did you find him?"

"No, I got a crayon."

"A crayon?"

"Yep. Move over."

"What're you doing?"

"I'm drawing a line down the middle of her bottom sheet."

"Is he supposed to walk along it?"

"No. It's for something else. Can you see it?"

Rog leaned over and ran his fingers up and down the sheet. "Yeah, it's right here."

"Okay," I said. "It's a boundary line, and that's your half over there. Don't you *dare* go past it."

13
Where Next?

Mom had lot to say about the crayon line on Snag's sheet the next morning. But I had bigger problems. And two days later they weren't any better.

All the commotion had convinced Wally that his one trip across Snag's bed was enough. Which was certainly understandable. Even high-tailing it right out of her room was understandable. But avoiding mine?

"My room's got to be next," Rog said.

"Or Mom and Dad's," I said.

The answer was sort of hanging in the air like the ending of the story of the lady or the tiger. And since our lives were at stake, we were definitely rooting for Roger's room instead of the alternative.

Meanwhile, droves of snoopy househunters had either seen the FOR SALE sign on our front lawn or the ads in the paper. Every time we turned around we bumped into somebody parading through the house.

Roger and I had to rely on Snag to tackle the job of getting rid of them, but I have to admit she was very good at it. Rudeness is her specialty . . . and while everybody was getting a sample, we were able to concentrate on Wally.

But Wally was sticking to his new hangout, wherever that was, and to add to the panic, time was running out till the Wigginses got home.

As hard as I tried, I couldn't get rid of this gnawing picture I had in my mind of how Billy was going to react when I broke the news to him:

"But, Michael, I thought you were supposed to be my friend," I could almost hear him saying. *"How could you lose Wally? My favorite pet? The world's most terrific lizard?"*

I wasn't up to carrying this picture a step further or thinking about the answer I'd be giving him. I was suffering enough as it was. And then, to make matters even worse, the first couple who'd seen our house came back to see it again, so I knew they *really* liked it.

The third time around, they brought a relative in the construction business to pound on the beams, flush the toilets, and feel for cracks. Mom told them to take their time inspecting everything, and she left them alone. But Snag raced upstairs ahead of them.

"Did you hear the creak?" she asked when she stopped to bounce on the third step.

"Yes," said the lady. "A dozen times yesterday."

"Did I ever tell you about the monster who lives in our walls?"

The three of them ignored her and marched single file into the first room they came to. It was Roger's, and, as usual, we were both in there looking for signs of Wally. None of the househunters even bothered to say "excuse me" when they saw us, so we didn't say anything to them, either. We just settled down on Roger's bed to play a game of Give-Away checkers and keep an eye on the clump of food we'd left by the wastepaper basket.

For a few minutes they talked about how a little imagination and good taste was going to turn the room into a cozy study. Then Mr. Construction Business breezed right by us and slid the windows open and shut a few times.

"I wouldn't do that too hard if I were you," Rog finally said.

"What's that, sonny?"

"Roger," said Roger. "R-O-G-E-R."

"Sorry, umm . . . Roger. Now what were you saying about the windows?"

"I said, 'I wouldn't do that too hard if I were you.'"

"Oh . . . why's that? Too drafty?"

"No. They usually fall right out . . . especially the ones in the kitchen. They're the worst." Rog paused and jumped one of my men. "Or do you think the ones in the living room are, Michael?"

Without stopping to look up, I went ahead and made my next move. "Oh, I don't know," I said, waiting for Rog to advance across the board. "They're all about the same by now. The termites must be everywhere."

Mr. Construction Business hustled his relatives out of Roger's room so fast they practically tripped over each other. "You can always count on kids," I heard him say when they got out in the hall. "They'll tell you the truth every time."

After they left we decided to replace Wally's bait, which was looking a little nauseating, and went outside to sneak a few fresh petals. When we got upstairs with them, Rog noticed that the clump we'd been watching was gone.

"He's in here, Michael," he said, squealing and hugging me. "Didn't I tell you . . . didn't I *know* he'd come in here next?" Both of us got down on the floor and started crawling around, calling, "Here, Pweshus . . . come on . . . come on out." Then Mom came by.

"No wonder the two of you wear the knees right out of your jeans. Are you looking for something?"

"A lost checker," I said, hiding the petals behind my back. "A black one."

"Hey, what d'ya know," said Rog. "There goes the doorbell. You'd better answer it, Mom."

"That's funny," she said, "I didn't hear it."

"Yeah . . . there it is again."

"Fourth time," I said.

Mom ducked out Rog's door, "Susan," she called, "would you mind getting the front door? If it's somebody to see the house, tell them I'll be down in a minute." Then she came back in. "By the way, did either of you say anything to those three people who were here a little while ago?"

"Just 'hello,' " I said.

"Just 'hello,' " echoed Roger. "And if I were you, *I* wouldn't let Susan answer the door by herself."

"Nobody's going to nab her," Mom told him, then she looked at me. "You're sure you didn't say anything else?"

"Positive."

"I'm *telling* you, Mom . . . those people are gonna be gone by the time you get downstairs."

"Roger, stop bugging me! Right now I'm more interested in why those *other* people left. Something sure scared them away, and if it wasn't anything you said, it was probably your garbage."

"*What* garbage?" we asked.

"You've been *eating* it, and you're asking *me?*" She took a deep breath. "Let's see now . . . there were slimy bananas, rotten grapes, wilted lettuce, mushy pears . . . and if I didn't know any better, I'd say the rest of it was decayed flowers. Every bit of it was caked on this rug, so from now on, NO MORE FOOD IN YOUR ROOMS! . . . And another thing," she said, stomping over to a window, "we're going to get some fresh air in here."

"DON'T," Rog screamed as she opened it. "Something might get out, I mean in . . . and anyway, I can't stand fresh air."

"Try it . . . your lungs might like it."

"*ALL RIGHT!*" We all looked at Snag who was standing in the doorway. "*All right,*" she repeated. "*Who's the wise guy?*"

"Wasn't anybody down there, dear?"

She pointed to us. "Ask *them.*"

"See," Rog said to Mom. "Didn't I tell you they'd be gone?"

"HA!"

Mom looked at her watch. "I didn't think Harriet would be by so early."

"Who's Harriet?" I asked.

"Mrs. Duvalier. She's coming in exactly ten minutes and I don't want any of you to say one word to her except 'hello' and 'good-bye.' "

14
The Lady from the Flower Show

Roger was so upset that it was Mom who'd snatched our bait, instead of Wally, he thought he needed a peanut butter sandwich and a brownie. I only wanted water, but I told him I'd go down to the kitchen to keep him company.

On our way, we looked through the living room window and saw a lady getting out of a long, black car. "Hey, I remember her," Rog said. "She comes to the flower shows, and she always wears her hair in a donut like that."

"Chignon," Mom barked as she hurried to the door, "and keep quiet." Then she swung the door open. "Why, Harriet, how nice to see you. Come on in."

By this time, Snag had slid down the banister and was straddled over the endpost. "Did you come to see our mole again, Mrs. . . . ummm, what'd you say her name was, Mom?"

"Mrs. Duvalier. And Susan . . . either go to your room or go outside while I take her through the house."

"But I showed her the burrow already . . . can't I just *tell* her the dragon walked across my bed?"

"NO!"

"*Awww,* not even what it looked like?"

Mrs. Duvalier studied Snag while Mom tried pulling her off the banister. "I didn't realize she was your child, Catherine. Does she hallucinate often?"

"Only when she wants to," Mom answered.

I hadn't exchanged two words with her yet, but somehow my instincts told me that Mrs. Duvalier was absolutely allergic to anyone under fifteen. Maybe even thirty. "You're gonna love this neighborhood," I told her. "It's *loaded* with kids."

"Yes," she said, turning to me and arching an eyebrow. "Aren't they all these days?"

Mom had finally gotten Snag off the banister and was shoving her out the door. "Come, Michael," she said rather sharply. "You and Roger are going outside too."

"I'm telling her about the neighborhood, Mom. You know . . . how kids are always playing in our yard, and climbing the trees?" I looked back at Mrs. Duvalier. "Do you have any children?"

"Only Chester," she said.

I was sort of surprised. "Oh . . . Chester? How big is he?"

"Eight inches. He's a Chihuahua."

I felt Mom's hand sink into my shoulder. "Come, dear . . . outside."

"Can I stay?" Rog asked. "I haven't said anything."

"OUT!"

When Dad came home at dinner time, Mom met him at the door and gave him an up-to-the-minute report on the house. The three of us kept our distance while she was still on the story of "that nice couple who'd been on the verge of buying." But after she finished telling him how they'd left in a hurry, we straggled out to hear about Harriet, who was so "extremely interested" she was going to speak to her lawyer about a contract.

"I think it's our backyard more than anything else, Harold. Especially the hill with the rock garden. She says she fell in love with it the first time she saw it."

"For any particular reason?" Dad asked.

"Well, she tells me she has visions of a waterfall coming out of the top and falling into a pond at the bottom. Can you believe *that*?"

Dad looked amused. "From Harriet Duvalier I'd believe almost anything . . . even a pagoda. But I'm amazed that this place is fancy enough for her."

"It isn't. We just happen to have the only rock hill in town. 'It's one of a kind,' she says, and she knows that for a fact because she's been looking for another one since she thought of the waterfall."

"What does she say about the house?"

"That some major changes will make it adequate for her Louis XIV collection."

"Hmmm . . . from her that sounds promising."

Rog couldn't contain himself any longer. "Who's Louis XIV?"

"A king in France," Dad said. "Way back in the seventeenth century."

"She collects kings?" Snag asked.

Mom sighed. "No, Susan, she collects furniture. It's copied after the kind Louis XIV had . . . and *please,* do me a favor . . . don't ask her about it when they come over on Sunday."

"On Sunday," I said. "Who's coming with her . . . Chester?"

"No, Ernest . . . her husband." Mom turned to Dad and muttered, "You can't imagine how obnoxious your children were today."

"Of course I can," he said. "And if they keep it up, we might lose a sale." He loosened his tie and eyed us one at a time. "I don't know if the three of you realize this or not, but if we don't get rid of *this* house we won't be getting the Greenbergs'. They've had two offers beside ours . . . so no funny stuff when the Duvaliers come over on Sunday. *Clear?*"

"Clear," we said in a chorus.

Once he seemed satisfied that he'd made his point, he put his arm around Mom and they walked toward the kitchen. "Speaking of obnoxious children," he said, lowering his voice till he thought we couldn't hear him, "you should've heard what Arnold Oates told me this afternoon."

Rog looked at me. "I didn't do anything. Did you?"

"Oh, dear," said Mom. "Not trouble at school! Which one is it . . . Michael or Roger?"

"Relax, Catherine. This is about Marvin."

"Marvin?" Rog whispered, wrinkling his nose. "Old goodie-two-shoes?"

"Marvin?" Mom asked.

"Yes, and it's a corker. It seems the town's model child has been hiding two tarantulas in his room."

Mom gasped. *"Live* ones?"

"The last I heard they were. He's also been keeping a snake. In his closet!"

Mom gasped again. "Good Lord. And to think how I've always worried about Michael being friendly with that Wiggins boy."

That Wiggins boy really hit me. "Oh, no. What day is it?" I asked Rog.

"Wednesday," he said.

"I mean, what *number* is it . . . the twenty-ninth?"

"The thirtieth, why?"

"In his postcard Billy said he was coming back on the third. Let's see, that's . . ."

Rog counted on his fingers. "Four days."

"Sunday," I said.

Four days. Only ninety-six hours to go, I kept thinking during dinner. Just five thousand, seven hundred and sixty minutes.

"Michael, you haven't done anything but pick at that chicken," Mom said finally. "Aren't you hungry?"

"Uh-uh."

She looked at Dad. "I still think we should take him in for a check-up. He hasn't been eating anything lately."

"Maybe his appetite will perk up when he hears about the surprise after dinner."

I'm sure it was pre-planned, and Mom and Dad had intentionally kept the "surprise" a big secret until we were all trapped inside a locked, moving car.

"Bet I know where we're going," Rog said. "To a drive-in movie."

"Nope," said Dad, as we sped across town. "We're taking you to see what we *hope* is our next home."

I dug a piece of gum out of my pocket and leaned against the back seat to unwrap it. Then I just sat and chewed and thought how bleak the future was going to be. In four days Billy was coming home to no Wally. On the same horrible day, Harriet Duvalier was buying our house so *she* could build a waterfall and *we* could move into the Greenbergs' place.

And where was that? In Westlake, where all the

new houses go up. Way over on the other side of the world. When we got there I looked out the window at the big, boxy white house with its scrawny young trees and long, flat yard. So *this* was what I'd be giving up my old neighborhood and my friends for. Some bargain.

Then I saw the address printed on the mailbox: 395 PETUNIA LANE.

About a split-second later, Roger was crying and Snag was yelling, *"THAT DOES IT! PETUNIA LANE. I'LL NEVER EVER GET A PENPAL!"*

15
Maybes

Rog and I were at the end of our ropes. It was find Wally or *else,* so we prowled, searched, and poked into anything big enough to hold a pea.

On Friday, when we were convinced we had to come up with something new, we invented a game called "Let's Pretend We're Chuckwallas." Skeeter came over on the double to join us, so we let him take his turn first and he wrote down seven places where he'd hide. But Wally wasn't in any of them.

Roger and I each came up with eight places, including Mom's curler bag, but we weren't any luckier with our lists than we'd been with Skeeter's.

After Skeeter had to go home, we thought we saw something zip behind the piano in the living room. Rog rushed to one end and I got to the other, but the piano was too close to the wall for either of us to reach behind it.

It was also too heavy to move, so we gave up struggling and decided if it really was Wally we'd seen, we'd just have to drive him out.

"Why don't you try 'The Blue Danube'?" Rog asked me. "The way you play it, nothing could stay back there."

I played it over and over, pumping on the pedals and banging on the keys, but nothing happened. Then Roger sat on the bench beside me and we tried a duet of "The Campbells Are Coming" with our knuckles.

"That's enough!" Mom called from the next room. "If you're dying to practice, you can both start taking lessons again. But right now I don't want to hear another note . . . I can't concentrate on what I'm doing." What she was doing was cleaning the house.

And she kept right on scrubbing and polishing up until dinner time. Rog and I practically had to be carted away from our chairs by the piano to go eat. Then the minute we sat down Snag started complaining non-stop about how dizzy she was from the smell of ammonia and wax. So Dad did the worst thing possible. He opened all the windows to air out the house.

Rob gobbled up his plate of roast lamb, while I

picked at mine, and the first chance we got, we left the table and went back to our chairs in the living room. It seemed like we sat in there for hours . . . just waiting. But nothing stirred from behind the piano.

As bedtime grew closer, we got more and more scared about the grim possibility that Wally had climbed out of one of the windows.

On Saturday morning we gave up on the inside of the house and started looking outside. There wasn't a sign of Wally in the tall grass under any of the windows, but we still nearly freaked out when Dad went over it with the lawn mower in the afternoon.

On Sunday, I woke up feeling so miserable and down in the dumps I couldn't even drink the glass of water I was having for breakfast. It was all I could do to prop my head in my hands and stare at my gloomy reflection in the top of the table. Making it through the rest of the day was going to be the toughest job I'd ever had.

"Maybe something will happen," Rog told me.

"Oh, sure . . . like what?"

"Mmmm, I don't know. Maybe the Wigginses won't come back . . . then you won't have to tell Billy."

"They *live* here, Roger. They have to come back."

"Maybe the Duvaliers will get a divorce and she'll move away."

"Forget it. It's not going to happen."

Rog was back with the Wigginses. "Maybe they'll

join the Navajos . . . you never can tell."

When he didn't come up with any more maybes, I knew we were sunk, because Roger has more maybes than anybody. I just sat there while he finished his plate of French toast and wondered if anything good would ever happen again. Then Mom came by and told us to give our rooms a last-minute inspection.

"I wish today had happened so long ago I wouldn't remember it," I said on our way upstairs.

Rog stopped and put his hand on my shoulder. "I hate to tell you this, Michael . . . but I don't think you're ever going to forget it. Even when you're eighty-five."

Before the Duvaliers arrived, Dad rounded us up for another one of his "no-monkey-business" lectures and a long string of things that were going to happen if we didn't listen to him. Then the big, black car pulled up.

"Look at *her,* everybody," said Snag. "She's still got on her robe."

"Burnoose," Mom said. "She got it in Morocco . . . and *now,* I want all three of you . . ."

"Why didn't her husband get one?"

"Oh, I don't know! Harold . . . *please,* would you take them out the back way while I answer the door?"

"I've got it," said Rog. He opened the door and scrambled down the steps. "Boy, you weren't kidding about the eight inches," he called to Harriet as she quickly scooped Chester off the walk. "Want us to watch him while you look around?"

"No, no. He always stays with us . . . and you mustn't touch him. He's afraid of children."

Snag wrestled her way out of Mom's stranglehold and ran outside. "I still think it looks like a robe," she said, circling around Harriet, "even if it does have a hood."

Harriet glanced back at Ernest. "See what I mean?"

"I thought they had another one," he whispered.

"Straight ahead." She nodded when she saw me.

Dad hurried out and gave them a quick "hello" and told them to go right in without him. Then he herded us into the backyard. "All right," he said, plunking down the croquet set. "Start playing."

"What if they stay for three hours?" I asked.

"Then play for three hours."

"*Awwww,*" whined Snag. "What if I trip over a wicket and break my leg?"

"Then lie on the grass and don't walk on it," he snapped, "because you're not coming inside."

"But it's boiling," Rog said. "What if we need water, or one of us has to go to the bathroom?"

Dad was downright cranky. "You can get all the water you need out of the hose, and as far as the bathroom is concerned . . . one time each, no more."

He left me in charge and as soon as he went inside, Snag announced she had to go to the bathroom. "Not now," I said. "You're not going to learn anything yet."

We took our time setting up the stakes and wickets and after Rog and Snag had flipped a coin to see who was going to be black, we lined up our balls and I told Snag she could go inside for her turn.

"What've you decided to tell Billy?" Rog asked while we were waiting.

"I'm not sure . . . probably the truth."

"Ah, you can do better than that. What about sending him a telegram? 'Dear Bill . . . stop . . . moving away . . . stop . . . will speak to you in December . . . stop.' " He sat down on the lawn beside me. "Maybe it doesn't have to be in those words exactly, but at least you wouldn't have to tell him in person." I tapped the toes of my sneakers together while the picture of Billy hearing the news flashed through my mind. "Or," Rog went on, "if you don't like that, we could always make him a scrapbook."

"A scrapbook?"

"Yeah . . . we can put in lots of stories and pictures. 'Remember Wally,' we could call it, and my diorama would make a good cover."

"How can we use your diorama? You didn't even finish it."

Roger's face got very long. "You don't have to rub it in," he said, swallowing hard. "I never had a chance to . . . but I will now, if you want."

"Don't, Rog."

"Don't finish it?"

"Sure, finish it. Just don't cry, okay?"

"Okay, well . . . uh . . ."

The back door banged and Snag came out. "What's happening?" I called.

"She says a veil came with that long thing she's got on, but she never uses it . . . hey, what's *he* crying about? Petunia Lane again?"

"Leave him alone," I said. "He hurt his leg."

"You'd better lie on the grass, Roger. Dad won't let you in the house with it."

"What were they talking about?" I asked.

"The fireplace. What's-her-name says she'd like it with a marble mantle."

"Anything else?"

"Well, the kitchen'll be okay if they put some tiles on the floor, and she says there's plenty of room for her microbes."

"Her *microbes?*"

"Yeah. What are they, anyway?"

"Tiny little animals you can't even see without a microscope. They cause diseases."

Rog pounded the grass with his mallet. "After all the cleaning Mom did to please that weirdo . . . *sniff* . . . and she comes up with something like that. Did Mom faint?"

"Uh-uh. She thought it was a wonderful idea. She even wants one."

"Now I've heard everything," he said, smacking the

ground so hard a clump of grass and dirt stuck to the end of his mallet. "Old Mrs. Clean herself wants a microbe. And what about Dad . . . I suppose he does too."

"Nope, he just said a kitchen wasn't complete without one these days. Then he gave me a dirty look and told me to get out."

"Knock it off, Roger," I said as he sprayed me with dirt.

"Oh, what's the use," he cried, throwing down the mallet. Then he rolled over on the grass, moaning and groaning about what lousy parents we had.

I looked at Snag. "You've got something twisted around somewhere . . . they couldn't have been talking about microbes."

"HA! I oughta know . . . I was standing right there. Harriet said 'microbe' just as plain as day She even said she'd have room for her microbe oven."

"OVEN?" Rog yelled. *She cooks them?*"

I couldn't stand it any longer. "Oh, for Pete's sake, they must've meant a microwave oven . . . so let's drop the whole subject."

"What's a microwave oven?"

"A contraption that'll cook things like a turkey or a roast in just a few minutes."

"Ohhhh, shoot," said Snag. "Is *that* all?"

None of us really felt like playing croquet, so we each had a drink from the hose and decided it was time for Roger to take his turn.

When he came back he told us that everybody was going through our bedrooms, and Harriet definitely wanted the partition down. "She says it chops up that big, 'spacious' room, and her Louis XIV junk would 'overpower' it . . . and there's something else, Michael. I just don't know how to tell you."

"Just tell me."

"You're sure now?"

"Go on."

"While they were in your closet they were all wondering why you kept Christmas tree lights and a sunlamp in there."

"Did anybody guess?" I asked.

"I couldn't hear everything . . . Chester was barking too much, but Mom was mad as blazes that you were using my train box to store three rocks."

Snag was a little puzzled by the whole report, but she seemed willing to go along with anything we did if it put a kink in the sale. "Good for you, Michael. That was a terrific idea . . . maybe they won't buy the house now."

"That's not going to stop them," said Rog. "What's-his-face wants to show Dad some drawings he has for the waterfall. It's gonna have some kind of a pump in it."

I looked at my watch. "Well . . . time for my turn."

"Hey, Michael," Snag said, when I was getting up,

"why *do* you have Christmas tree lights in your closet?"

"So I can plug in the sun-lamp."

As I walked away, I heard her quizzing Roger about the sun-lamp. "I'm not really sure," he told her, "but I think he uses it to warm up his robe on cold mornings."

16
It Really Was Happening

When I came in the house I knew the second-floor tour was over, because Chester was yapping out in the living room. It seemed like a waste of time to make a trip to the bathroom since nobody was upstairs, so I stayed in the kitchen to listen.

"This is the electric pump under the pond over here," Ernest was saying. "It'll force the water up through these pipes and we can recirculate it."

My stomach was growling and even though I didn't feel like eating, I needed something to quiet it down. I poured myself a glass of milk and reached for the cookie jar. Darn Roger, I thought as I felt the strawberry pinwheel crumbs on the bottom, he never leaves anything.

Then I heard Harriet laughing. "Chester thinks

your cookies are divine, Catherine. See how he's sitting up begging for another one?"

I stomped over to the refrigerator. No pie. No cake. Just the usual bottles and jars and the leftover leg of lamb roast.

". . . and you simply *must* promise me that you and Harold will be the first to come see it when we're finished. The pond should be absolutely *glor*ious when it's filled with lilies and goldfish." Chester yapped again. "There you go," Harriet said to him. "You just can't get enough of them, can you, darling?"

I've never eaten a lamb sandwich and I probably never would've tried fixing one then, if I hadn't been stalling for time in the kitchen. Almost automatically, I reached for the bread and pulled out two slices. Then I sawed into the roast and strained my ears to hear Dad telling Ernest how he and Mom had bought our house right after they were married.

". . . it seemed like a wonderful place to raise a family. To this day we feel we made the right decision."

"Is that so?" Ernest offered.

"Yes, we've all been happy here. Every room is filled with special memories . . ." Dad paused, clearing his throat. "It'll be eight years next month since our two boys . . ."

I looked down at the gray slab of meat I'd just sliced off the bone, and I felt my stomach tighten. It was even grayer looking once I'd slapped it onto a piece of white bread. Ahh, what's the use, I thought as I squashed the whole thing up in my hand. Then my eyes started stinging and I shut them tight.

". . . waiting to see their new sister for the first time," Dad's voice trailed back in, "and they were just standing there with their noses pressed against the window . . ."

"Oh, Harold," interrupted Harriet. "I'm so glad you mentioned windows. Did Ernest tell you about our first major change in the house?"

"No, I don't believe he did."

"Tell him, darling."

"Well," began Ernest, "we'd like to knock out that back wall and put in either a huge window or sliding glass doors."

"Neither really," Harriet continued. "We prefer to think of it as a way of opening up the living room and extending it to our backyard. We want to *experience* our oasis as if it were a changing, lyrical painting . . . a microcosm of nature that *we've* created and brought into *this* room."

The milk gurgled as I poured it in the sink and a bubble formed over the drain.

"No, thank you," Dad said as papers began rattling. "I've got a pen in my pocket."

Except for Chester's constant yapping, it grew very quiet out in the living room. "Let's see," said Ernest, "now that we've agreed to the terms in this contract, why don't we go ahead and sign these two copies?"

I braced myself against the sink, too numb to move. Somewhere deep inside me, I'd never truly believed it would happen . . . but it was. Less than thirty feet from the very spot where I was standing, the only house I'd ever known was being sold.

"Well, it's done," Mom said. "And I must admit I'm relieved about having sixty days until the closing date. It's going to take longer than we expected for the children to get used to the idea of moving. After all, they're very attached to this neighborhood."

Ernest offered another one of his "is that so's," then he said, "well, if those boys of yours get homesick for their old house here . . . send them right over. We'll give them a job doing all the yard work for us."

I started to carry the lamb roast back to the refrigerator, but stopped halfway across the room when I heard Harriet pick up on the yard work. "Darling," she said, "don't forget they're *not* professional gardeners. I think you should make that quite clear when you speak to them about it."

"What would you suggest . . . fifty cents to mow the lawn, and maybe a dollar a day for both of them to do the weeding and watering?"

"That's *more* than adequate," she answered dryly. "But since you've already quoted those figures as wages, we can't be unfair and back down."

There was something so slick about the way the two

of them had maneuvered Mom's comment about moving into a discussion of cheap labor. Like they'd written the lines out ahead of time and knew just how they were going to worm them in. Then they had the nerve to sit out there acting like they were doing us a favor!

"Catherine," said Harriet, "it would be a marvelous idea if you and Harold gave your boys some gardening tips and a little training before you move. . . ."

"Yes," Ernest added with a forced laugh, "as a preventive measure, you might say."

The more he laughed and the more Chester yapped, the harder it was for me to fight back my tears. I would never cut a single blade of grass for them! Not in a thousand years! And neither would Rog!

"You can get somebody else to do your dirty work," I said, walking out into the living room.

I waited for some kind of reaction, but nobody even looked up. At one end of the coffee table, Dad and Ernest were huddled over a pile of papers, discussing mortgages and lawyers. At the other end, Mom was pouring a cup of tea for Harriet who was sitting across from her, facing me.

Chester lifted his nose off her lap and began sniffing the air in my direction. "Listen," I said as he zeroed in on the leg of lamb I'd forgotten I was holding, "you can get . . ."

His yapping drowned out the rest of my sentence and Harriet reached for the last pinwheel. When Chester had snapped it up, she took the cup of tea Mom had been holding for her and set it down next to a large vase of prize Spitfires and skimpy Talismans. "As you know, Catherine," she said, stirring in some sugar, "we travel so much, and it's simply not safe to be abroad these days with one's valuables sitting in a showplace. Somebody breaks in . . . and poof, they're gone." She placed her spoon on the saucer. "This is just what we need . . . a modest, inconspicuous house."

I saw Mom's back stiffen. "Cream?" she asked.

It was finally quiet enough for me to get a word in. "Listen," I repeated, "you can get somebody . . ."

"Good Lord," Harriet gasped when she looked up and saw the lamb. "What a barbaric . . ."

I'll never know what else she said because I suddenly noticed something under her chair moving toward the table. From the look in its beady eyes, I knew it was dead set on getting to the Talismans, and it was going to waddle right between her feet to do it.

"Michael," Mom said, turning to me, "what in the world are you doing in here with that . . ."

"OOOH, MY LORRRD," Harriet bellowed. "OOOOOOOH, MY LORRRRRD!" Everyone looked at her. "OOOOOOH . . . OOOOOOH . . . OOOOOOH, MY LOOOORRD!"

"What's the matter?" yelled Ernest.

She pointed down at Wally who was puffed up between her ankles. "LOOK . . . YOU SEE IT?

OHHHH, MY LORRRRD . . . IT'S GOING TO ATTACK!"

"He won't hurt you," I told her, "but I think you're scaring him."

Chester was howling and whimpering, and she clutched him against her chest and climbed to the top of her chair. "Don't move," Ernest shouted, "we'll get it with something." Then he turned to me. "Find a broom!"

"We don't have one," I said, glancing at Mom who was staring straight ahead as if she was nailed to the back of her chair. "Don't worry, Mom . . . he couldn't bite her if he wanted to. Honest. He doesn't have teeth."

Ernest grabbed the leg of lamb from my hand and held it out to Dad. "Do something, Harold . . . beat it with this."

"Give it back," I yelled, taking it away from him. "I'm eating it."

Chester yelped and Harriet stomped her foot on the arm of the chair. "SSSTT . . . SCAT . . . SSST . . . SCAT . . . SCAT!"

"What is it, Michael?" Dad asked.

"A chuckwalla. Billy Wiggins' chuckwalla . . . he's harmless and he's been lost . . . and *please* . . . don't let anybody hurt him."

"Give me that thing," Ernest commanded.

I held the leg of lamb behind my back and he shook

Dad's arm. "Harold, do *something!* Get a gun, call the police . . ."

The back door slammed and Roger came tearing in with Snag at his heels. "What's going on? We heard all this screaming in here and we . . . WALLY! WALLY . . . IT'S YOU!" Rog jumped up and down, clapping. "Michael, it's *really* Wally." I nodded and he gave me a squeeze. "Isn't this just terrific?"

"Hey . . . wait a minute," Snag said. "That's the same . . ."

"Take him out of here, Michael," Dad cut in.

I scurried around the side of the coffee table, trying to dodge Harriet's shoulder bag as she smacked it against the legs of her chair. Snag had already crawled under the table from the other side and we reached Wally at the same time. "Michael," she whispered, "he's not nearly as scary in the daytime." Then she held her hand out to him. "See," she called up to Harriet. "You can come down now . . . he won't bite."

"You *brat,*" Harriet sputtered. "Loathsome, uncivilized *brats* . . . all of you. I should've known you'd pull some kind of . . ." She glared at Dad and stamped her foot again. "Ohh, get those brats and that *thing* away from me!"

"Do *shut* up," Dad told her.

I reached for Wally.

"No wonder these children don't have any manners," Ernest said, as he gathered up the papers. "The fruit *never* falls far from the tree."

"Come on," I called to Roger and Snag as I stroked poor, frightened, shaky Wally.

Rog followed me, but Snag inched her way out from under the table and then stood in front of Harriet's chair. "If you ask me, Harriet Duvalier, you're the one who's uncivilized. We'd *never ever* walk all over somebody else's furniture."

I think Snag was about up to the word "never" when Harriet took a swipe at her, and she had to start running. Somehow she managed to make it past the table, but the shoulder bag kept right on sailing into the vase of flowers.

A little color came back into Mom's face, and as we flew out of the room, I saw her rising slowly from her chair.

17
The Telephone Call

There was so much shouting and yelling and yapping going on in the living room, I hardly knew which way to turn once we got out of there. "Here," I said, quickly plopping Wally into Roger's arms, "watch him, and don't let anybody at him. I'm gonna try and reach Billy."

He darted up the stairs and I ran to the kitchen to use that phone, since it's the closest, but by the time I picked it up I'd already blanked out on Billy's number. I couldn't even remember the one for information, so I had to start by dialing the operator. When I'd finally worked my way up to information, the noise in the living room had gotten louder and louder. "Would you mind repeating that number please," I said. "I'm standing in the middle of a bowling alley."

"EV 6-9301."

"EV 6-9301, EV 6-9301," I kept saying over and over as I hung up and tried stretching the cord to the broom closet. "EV 6-9301." The cord wouldn't go that far, so I opened a cabinet near the stove and crawled in. "EV 6-9301."

The phone rang and rang before Billy answered. "Well, what d'ya know," he said, when he got on the line, "I was just coming in from the greenhouse so I could call *you*. Now how's that for mental telepathy?"

"Pretty good," I said. "When did you get home?"

"A couple of hours ago. And say . . . don't keep me in suspense . . . how've things been going with Wally?"

I crawled farther into the cabinet so only my feet were sticking out. "Fine," I said, hoping he couldn't hear the front door banging and a car squealing out of our driveway. "He really made a hit. The whole family was crazy about him."

"Wow! I knew it . . . I just *knew* it! Isn't the mind amazing?"

"Amazing," I answered.

"Michael, you wouldn't believe this feeling I had on our trip. I could actually *see* you guys with Wally . . . and everything was perfect. I'll tell you all about it when you come over with him."

"I can bring him over now if you want," I said as I saw Snag walk around my feet and head for the refrigerator. "I'm *positive* Mom and Dad won't mind."

"Stupendous! Why don't you plan on staying a while? I'll teach you this Navajo song that I learned."

Snag pulled a tray of ice out of the freezer and walked around my feet again. "Song?" I asked.

"That's right! A real Navajo song and it's *in* Navajo. You're gonna love it . . . Michael? . . . Hello? . . . (click, click) . . . Michael, are you still there?"

"Yeah, I'm still here."

"Oh, good. For a minute I thought we'd been disconnected."

"No, I was just thinking, that's all."

"Wait . . . don't tell me. You were thinking you were just in the mood for the song, right?"

"Right," I said, "but don't you . . ."

"Don't worry. I've got plenty of time . . . I'll even teach you the dance that goes along with it."

"In the greenhouse?"

"Sure, that'll be a great place."

"But isn't it going to be crowded? What about Skeeter bringing over the chameleons, and Marvin with the tarantulas . . ."

"Aww, they're all coming back tomorrow . . . except for the tarantulas and snake. We've got to pick them up at the A.S.P.C.A."

"What do you mean, the A.S.P.C.A.? I thought Marvin had them."

"So did I till we got a telegram. Can you believe his

father actually had it delivered right up to the reservation?"

"Really?"

"Really! And that's the last time I ever let *him* take care of anything. D'ya know he didn't even tell his folks? They didn't know a thing until one of the tarantulas got loose . . . then his mother nearly had a bird. She thought it was poisonous."

"No kidding?"

"Yeah, some story, huh?"

"Yeah . . . See you in a little while," I said, hanging up.

I stayed in the cabinet for a few minutes, because I didn't dare move until I was certain the row was over in the living room. When I finally realized it was dead quiet, I took a peek in there and saw that everybody had cleared out. Even the flowers were gone. The only thing left was a broken vase lying in a puddle of water.

"Roger?" I shouted and dashed upstairs.

18
"Ernest Was Right"

"**W**e're in my room," Rog called when he heard me coming.

His door was partially open, and when I got to the landing I could see Snag sitting on his bed sorting through some shredded papers. "Since what's-her-name's not putting in the waterfall," she was saying, "why don't we do it?"

"No, thank you. I can do without microcosms of nature in my backyard."

The second voice was Dad's. It took me by surprise to hear him still speaking to any of us, but I was twice as surprised when I walked in and found him sprawled out on the floor with Roger.

And I was even more surprised when I saw him feeding Wally some petals. "Little crunchers, you say? Fascinating creature, isn't he?"

I sat down beside them while Roger showed him how Wally loved to be stroked under his chin. "Feel him, Dad. Isn't he soft? Maybe it's because he doesn't sweat."

Dad ran his hand down Wally's back. Then he stopped and looked at me, and when he did, I had a hunch his mental telepathy was a lot better than Billy's. "Don't worry," he said, "they've left."

"The Duvaliers?"

He nodded.

"I'm . . . I'm sorry, Dad. I really am. They weren't very nice to you and Mom."

"Or us," said Roger.

"Or the furniture," Snag said.

Dad kept a steady gaze on me as he held out another petal for Wally. "You don't have to apologize, Michael. Certainly not for their behavior. How were you to know that Billy's long-lost pet was going to upset the applecart?"

"I knew he was lost . . . I guess it's my fault for not telling you."

"Never mind. We'll talk about that some other time. I'm not up to the whole story just yet."

"Dad's right, Michael," Rog blurted out. "It'd be a good idea if you waited."

I looked at both of them. "Okay . . . if you think so."

"As a matter of fact," Dad continued, "why don't we all just remember Wally's debut today as an act of fate? As far as I'm concerned, no one could have predicted his timing under that chair."

"Right," said Roger. "Not even Michael."

Snag glanced over at me and I thought she was going to say something, but she only grinned and then went back to sorting out her papers.

"Where's Mom?" I asked.

"Resting."

"Is she going to be all right?"

"When she gets rid of her headache."

"I mean, is she upset, Dad? She really wanted to sell this house."

Dad smiled. "The Duvaliers aren't the only people in the world who buy houses."

"Oh, now I get it," groaned Roger. "You're planning on showing the house again."

"Probably . . . but not for a while. Your mother says it'll be ten years before she can go through this all over again."

"What about the Greenbergs?" Snag asked. "Do you think they're going to wait around that long?"

"No, but then their house won't be the last one on the market, either. There'll be more."

"Not like theirs . . . you said so yourself, Daddy. I heard you. You said you and Mommy loved it."

"Not exactly, Susan. I liked it. I thought it was big and roomy. Your mother was the one who loved it."

I watched Wally climb up to Roger's shoulder and sit there like they'd never been separated a day in their lives. "Speaking of Mom," I said, "maybe she'll cheer up a bit if I tell her I'm taking Wally back to Billy's."

"Can I go over with you?" Rog asked a little sadly.

"Sure. Why don't you see if you can find something to carry him in while I talk to Mom."

"Okay . . . meet me down in the garage. Maybe there's an extra gunnysack lying around."

The shades were drawn in Mom and Dad's bedroom, so I stood by the doorway till my eyes got used to the darkness. Then I tiptoed over to the quiet, motionless figure stretched out on top of the bed. "Mom," I whispered," are you awake?"

"YES, UNFORTUNATELY!" she answered.

"Well, I . . . I just wanted you to know how sorry we are . . . I am, about what happened."

She lifted the icebag off her head and sat up. "Did you *ever* . . . ever in your life see such appalling people?"

"I thought you liked them."

"*Liked* them? *Me?* Good heavens, no. Your father was just so set on buying the Greenbergs' house . . . and I was only trying to be polite. Believe me, Michael, *it was a job!*"

She dropped her head back on the pillow and replaced the icebag. "A grown woman like Harriet, attacking an eight-year-old child with her pocketbook.

Why . . . it's just mind-boggling!"

I stood quietly by the side of the bed and she lifted a corner of the icebag off one eye so she could look at me. "Do you know, they actually planned to *use* you and Roger . . . like you were a couple of serfs who came with the house?"

I nodded.

"Oh, you heard, then. Did you see the strawberry jam that was all over the chair after she got through stuffing her overgrown mouse?"

I nodded, even though I hadn't noticed the jam.

"Then I guess you must've heard what I said to them when they left."

"Uh-uh. I didn't see them leave."

"That's good. It wasn't the kind of language children should hear . . . especially from a parent. She deserved *every* word of it, though . . . the old PHONY!"

"Phony" shot off the tip of Mom's tongue like a missile, then she sighed a long sigh, and slid the icebag back to the center of her forehead.

"Mom," I said softly, "there's something I wanted to tell you. Remember Wally . . . the lizard? The one who was lost?"

"Is *he* still in this house?"

"Well, that's what I wanted to tell you. I'm taking him back over to Billy Wiggins' the minute Roger finds something to carry him in. Is there anything I can get you before we leave?"

"No, thank you, dear. I just want to lie here till my head stops thobbing."

I was almost to the door when she called me back. "Michael, would you do me one favor?"

"Sure."

"Don't eat in the living room anymore, okay? Not even . . . well, whatever it was you had."

"I promise."

"And another thing. Do tell Billy to be more careful with his reptiles. I wouldn't want another one to come calling on us."

"I'll tell him," I said.

"Be sure now. Once is enough."

As I was closing the door, I heard her suddenly burst out laughing. "Mom," I said, peering back in, "you're sure you're all right?"

She sat up and wiped her eyes with a tissue. "It's nothing," she answered, then started laughing again like she was never going to quit.

"You're sure?"

"I'm sure."

"You need some aspirin?"

"No, I'm fine . . . really. It's just something Ernest said. It struck me funny."

"*Ernest?*"

She nodded. "About the fruit never falling far from the tree."

"What's so funny about that . . . didn't he mean we

were like you and Dad?"

"Maybe he did," she said, "but while he was saying it, Chester was yowling right along with Harriet . . ."

Mom broke up all over again and I waited until she was able to go on.

"Oh, I know this is going to sound positively fiendish, Michael . . . but at the time, I couldn't help thinking that in *their* case, Ernest was right."

19
The World's Most Terrific Lizard

When I was going downstairs, I started thinking how you never really know the people you live with sometimes. And you never really know, for certain, how things are going to turn out.

From the moment Harriet saw Wally, there wasn't one person in my family who hadn't said or done something to surprise me. Except for Rog. He'd been his old usual, one hundred percent, true-blue predictable self, and that's a pretty comforting thing to know about somebody on the kind of day we'd just lived through.

Not that I was upset with the way all the unexpected events turned out. It's just that they reminded me of a long talk I had with Dad last year, when everybody was leaving for camp.

"I know you're disappointed because you're not going," he told me as we watched the millionth chicken pox erupt on my body. "But there are times when each of us has to cope with the unexpected."

I guess I'd always understood him to mean that unexpected things that happen were always going to be worse than expected things that *don't* happen. That morning, June 3rd, I woke up expecting the world to come to an end, and it hadn't. So I knew unexpected events sometimes turn out better. And I knew that for sure when I walked into the garage.

Roger was sitting on the fender of the car holding Wally, and he didn't hear me come in. "You'll neber know how worried Unka Rogie was," he was telling him. "I thought maybe you didn't like us anymore. But you came back . . . just when we needed you the most."

For a minute he ran his finger along Wally's back and down his tail. Then he bent down his head and rubbed him with his cheek. "And I'll neber forget it, Pweshus. Neber."

I gave a little cough and Rog looked up. "Time, huh?"

"Afraid so," I answered.

"If you don't mind, Michael . . . do you think you could put him in the gunnysack by yourself? I don't want to watch."

"Sure," I said, taking Wally from him. Then I picked up the sack that was on his lap and lowered

Wally to the bottom. Billy's right, I thought, he *is* the world's most terrific lizard.

I tapped Rog. "Well . . . we're ready."

He opened his eyes and looked at the sack. "After all he did for us," he sighed. Then he hopped off the fender. "But at least he's in there and that's more than we've been counting on."

We strolled out of the garage carrying Wally between us, and I started thinking how our house was going to be back to normal soon. I'd miss Wally. That was for sure.

Still, it'd be a relief knowing that he was safe and sound in his greenhouse.

"You know what I was wondering?" Rog asked.

I shook my head.

"I was wondering what Billy brought you from Arizona."

"Oh, yeah . . . the surprise. I'd almost forgotten about that. Didn't he say the picture on the postcard was supposed to be a hint?"

Rog nodded. "Think it's the sheep?"

"Uh-uh. The basket."

"Well," he shrugged, "who knows? Maybe it'll be a wonderful basket. Maybe it'll be so wonderful you'll learn to love baskets."

I wasn't so sure I'd ever learn to love this basket, or any other basket, but it would always remind me of the things that happened while Wally was with us. I promised myself that whenever I looked at it, I'd try to remember that the worst doesn't always come to the worst.

"What are you going to do with it?" Rog asked.

I thought about it for a minute, then I looked at him. "How'd you like to go fifty-fifty with me on the basket, since you've been fifty-fifty with me on Wally?"

"Really?"

"Really. I mean it, Rog. You stuck it out every inch of the way. Like those guys in that saying at the post office. The ones you can always count on . . . through rain or snow, or heat or gloom of night. You're like one of them."

Rog couldn't stop smiling. "Y'know, Michael," he said as we tried steadying the sack so it wouldn't swing too much, "today didn't turn out to be so bad after all. Maybe we won't *mind* thinking about it when we're eighty-five."

I didn't have the heart to tell him that we were going to be whooping it up, singing and dancing, in the greenhouse before the day was over. "Maybe," I said, keeping it to myself, "you never can tell."

We walked past the lilac bushes that border our driveway, and I took a deep breath. For as long as I could remember, their smell always meant summer to me.

And the best part was, we'd still be in our house when they bloomed again next year. . . .

Thanks to Wally.

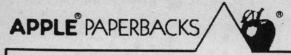

APPLE® PAPERBACKS

Pick an Apple and Polish Off Some Great Reading!

BEST-SELLING APPLE TITLES

❏ MT43944-8	**Afternoon of the Elves** Janet Taylor Lisle	$2.75
❏ MT43109-9	**Boys Are Yucko** Anna Grossnickle Hines	$2.75
❏ MT43473-X	**The Broccoli Tapes** Jan Slepian	$2.95
❏ MT42709-1	**Christina's Ghost** Betty Ren Wright	$2.75
❏ MT43461-6	**The Dollhouse Murders** Betty Ren Wright	$2.75
❏ MT43444-6	**Ghosts Beneath Our Feet** Betty Ren Wright	$2.75
❏ MT44351-8	**Help! I'm a Prisoner in the Library** Eth Clifford	$2.75
❏ MT44567-7	**Leah's Song** Eth Clifford	$2.75
❏ MT43618-X	**Me and Katie (The Pest)** Ann M. Martin	$2.75
❏ MT41529-8	**My Sister, The Creep** Candice F. Ransom	$2.75
❏ MT42883-7	**Sixth Grade Can Really Kill You** Barthe DeClements	$2.75
❏ MT40409-1	**Sixth Grade Secrets** Louis Sachar	$2.75
❏ MT42882-9	**Sixth Grade Sleepover** Eve Bunting	$2.75
❏ MT41732-0	**Too Many Murphys** Colleen O'Shaughnessy McKenna	$2.75

ADVENTURE! MYSTERY! ACTION!

Exciting stories for you!

☐ MN42417-3	The Adventures of the Red Tape Gang	Joan Lowery Nixon	$2.75
☐ MN41836-X	Custer and Crazy Horse: A Story of Two Warriors	Jim Razzi	$2.75
☐ MN44576-6	Encyclopedia Brown Takes the Cake!		$2.95
	Donald J. Sobol and Glenn Andrews		
☐ MN42513-7	Fast-Talking Dolphin	Carson Davidson	$2.75
☐ MN42463-7	Follow My Leader	James B. Garfield	$2.75
☐ MN43534-5	I Hate Your Guts, Ben Brooster	Eth Clifford	$2.75
☐ MN44113-2	Kavik, the Wolf Dog	Walt Morey	$2.95
☐ MN32197-8	The Lemonade Trick	Scott Corbett	$2.95
☐ MN44352-6	The Loner	Ester Weir	$2.75
☐ MN41001-6	Oh, Brother	Johnniece Marshall Wilson	$2.95
☐ MN43755-0	Our Man Weston	Gordon Korman	$2.95
☐ MN41809-2	Robin on His Own	Johnniece Marshall Wilson	$2.95
☐ MN40567-5	Spies on the Devil's Belt	Betsy Haynes	$2.75
☐ MN43303-2	T.J. and the Pirate Who Wouldn't Go Home	Carol Gorman	$2.75
☐ MN42378-9	Thank You, Jackie Robinson	Barbara Cohen	$2.95
☐ MN44206-6	The War with Mr. Wizzle	Gordon Korman	$2.75
☐ MN42378-9	Thank You, Jackie Robinson	Barbara Cohen	$2.95
☐ MN44206-6	The War with Mr. Wizzle	Gordon Korman	$2.75
☐ MN44174-4	The Zucchini Warriors	Gordon Korman	$2.95

Available wherever you buy books, or use this order form.

Scholastic Inc., P.O. Box 7502, 2931 East McCarty Street, Jefferson City, MO 65102

Please send me the books I have checked above. I am enclosing $_____ (please add $2.00 to cover shipping and handling). Send check or money order — no cash or C.O.D.s please.

Name _____

Address _____

City _____ State/Zip _____

Please allow four to six weeks for delivery. Offer good in the U.S. only. Sorry, mail orders are not available to residents of Canada. Prices subject to change.

AB991